Favorite

Favorite

KAREN MCQUESTION

PUBLISHED BY

amazonencore

The characters and events portrayed in this book are fictitious. Any similarity to real persons, living or dead, is coincidental and not intended by the author.

Published by AmazonEncore
P.O. Box 400818
Las Vegas, NV 89140

ISBN-13: 9781935597254
ISBN-10: 1935597256

For Mom, who said *Favorite* was her favorite

Acknowledgments

I'm grateful to my editor, Terry Goodman, who made it possible for me to write full time when he invited me to become an AmazonEncore author. You're my hero, Terry! Try to remember that even when I'm giving you grief.

Marketing expert Sarah Tomashek works hard to make her authors look good. All of us appreciate it, but I appreciate it the most. Secretly I think she likes me best.

I am indebted to Jessica Smith, who is one excellent copyeditor. If there are any errors in this book, it's my fault, not hers. On occasion she tried to set me right and I just wouldn't listen. I'm like that sometimes.

A special thank you to Amazon and AmazonEncore for being forward thinking and a true partner to me as an author. I look forward to future collaborations.

This novel went through extensive changes over the years. Those who helped steer it toward its final version include Vickie Coats, Kay Ehlers, Geri Erickson, Alice L. Kent, Felicity Librie, Katie Memmel, Anita Miller of Academy Chicago Publishers, Jeannée Sacken, Ben Salmon, Michelle Schrubbe, Rachel Sievers, and Neela Sukhatme-Sheth. Thanks to all.

To my family—Greg, who always believed in me, and our kids, Charlie, Maria, and Jack, who challenged me and made me laugh. You four are definitely my favorites.

Chapter 1

My dad claims to be psychic. He says things like, "I had a good feeling you'd ace that exam, Angie. I could have told you so." Last year he said he knew I'd get a part in the school play, and recently he told me he'd been absolutely sure my older brother would get the summer job he'd applied for at a landscape company. This was after both things had already happened. My dad's accuracy is uncanny; it's his timing that needs work. Still, if he says he gets these flashes of insight, I believe him. He's a very truthful guy.

I'd like to be able to say that I inherited some of his ability, but it's not true. My friends and I once played this game where you shuffle cards, put them face down, and then try to guess the number and color. I never got close, not even once. So clearly I'm not psychic, which sucks for me since there are times I'd give anything to have that particular talent, like every minute of every single day since my eleventh birthday.

I turned sixteen this past March, and my summer job was with a commercial cleaning firm, which meant I cleaned office buildings on Saturdays and evenings. Most of my friends thought it would be creepy working in empty buildings, but it didn't bother me. I just listened to my music and did what I needed to do.

The first Saturday of summer vacation, Grandma got up early to go golfing with Arthur and left the Honda for me to take to work. After eating breakfast, I filled my cat's food bowl, grabbed my water bottle, and put our vacuum cleaner in the trunk just in case the one at Midwest Technologies crapped out on me again. My plan for the morning was to pick up my grandmother's silk dress from the dry cleaner's first and then head off to work.

The dry cleaning place in my neighborhood strip mall was like any other you'd find in small-town Wisconsin, right down to the chemical smells, the silver countertop bell, and the clothes rod mounted next to the register. I still had the receipt from when I'd dropped off Grandma's dress a few days before. In one short week, when she married Arthur, it would become her wedding dress. Their engagement had been a big shocker for my older brother Jason and me. We had assumed they were just friends, but we were wrong. Who knew? Now Arthur and Grandma were getting married, and the three of us were moving out of our apartment and into his condo, which was going to be weird, but at least it was close enough so we wouldn't have to switch schools.

No one was in sight at the dry cleaner's when I walked in, but I sensed movement in the back of the building. The loud headbanger music coming from the rear reminded me of the heavy metal thumping I'd heard so often from Jason's room.

I tapped the bell twice. A girl came out, took my receipt without comment, and pushed the button to turn the rotating rack of clothes. Her eyes were still on the receipt when she returned, hanger in hand. "Hey," she said as she hung the dress on the rod in front of me, "your last name is 'Favorite.' That's kinda cool."

I nodded. I've heard it all by now—I must be everybody's favorite, maybe I'm nobody's favorite, was I my *mother's* favorite? That one always made me want to cry.

"And your first name starts with A." Her head bobbed in approval. "A. Favorite." She said it slowly, as if trying out a foreign phrase. "Way cool." She punched a few buttons on the register and ran the scanner over the tag. "Kind of like you're going through life as a chosen one. Like in the Bible."

Now *that* one I hadn't heard before. "Yep, that's me," I said. "The chosen one." A strand of hair had escaped my ponytail. I tucked it behind my ear before handing her a twenty-dollar bill. If I wanted to I could have kept the conversation going by telling her that my first initial actually stood for "Angel," but I decided not to go there.

She rifled through the register drawer and gave me my change in one lump. She said, "You have a good day now," in a really happy way.

It wasn't until I was out in my car that I looked at the wad of cash in my hand and realized she had given me the wrong amount. Math was not my best subject, but I knew if you paid someone with a twenty and got a twenty, a single, and some quarters in return, something wasn't adding up. My first thought was to just let it go. I sat for a moment, staring at the cash and thinking of the girl's earnest face and her friendly voice, and then I sighed. I had to take the money back. I didn't want her to get into trouble because of me.

I tossed my wallet on the front seat of the car and got out with car keys and money in hand, not even bothering to lock the door. The Honda was the only car in the lot and just twenty feet from the front of the store. I figured it would only take a minute.

I was almost to the curb separating the parking lot from the storefront sidewalk when I glanced up, startled to see a dark-haired man coming toward me. He didn't appear menacing at first. Just big. At least a foot taller than me, he had the bulky look of someone who wrestled professionally. He stepped off the curb as I approached. I mumbled a hello, but he didn't seem to notice.

The next part I remember as if I'm watching a movie and seeing it happen to someone else. I'm lost in my thoughts, money clutched in one hand, the car keys in the other, and I'm walking toward the dry cleaner's as if pulled by a string. The spell was broken when my arm was grabbed from behind. Shocked, I turned toward the guy whose vise-grip had stopped me.

I blurted out, "What do you want?" and looked to see if there was anyone else around, but we were alone. When I first passed him, I hadn't noticed anything but his size. Now I saw that his forehead was slick with sweat, and his sunken brown eyes were so dark in color they looked like two big pupils. I thought maybe he'd mistaken me for someone else until he grunted three words: "Come with me."

It all happened so fast—I've heard people use that expression before, but I never really knew what it meant until right at that moment. Because it did happen that fast. In an instant I thought of the girls you hear about in the news, the ones who were abducted and raped, and how they tell you never to go anywhere with an attacker unless you want to end up dead.

"Let go." I tried to scream the words, but they came out as a strangled cry. I pulled away from him, but he held fast. I always wondered how I'd react if I were attacked. Now I knew. I had assumed I'd scream loud enough to rouse the dead and would kick or punch his eyes, neck, or groin, like they tell you to do, but I didn't know it was going to be like this. I couldn't get away from him, and I was afraid. Scary movies, roller coasters, nightmares—nothing compared to the heart-pounding terror I felt at that moment.

"You need to see something," he said, his voice flat. "Come with me."

Tears came to my eyes and I tried to break free, but at 115 pounds I wasn't any match for his size and strength. He dragged me the length of the parking lot and past the other stores—the title insurance company, the Chinese restaurant, the gift shop. None of the businesses were open yet.

The whole time he just kept going as if he'd been programmed. At some point I dropped the money and then my car keys. I remember the plinking of coins as they bounced off the pavement like hail and the keys glinting in the early morning light.

I looked back at Grandma's car, and the sight of it made me think about the wallet I'd left in plain sight on the front seat. So stupid of me. If I disappeared, would someone find it and look for me? Or would someone steal it, removing the evidence I'd once been there?

Over and over again, I tried to catch my breath, but I couldn't get a lungful. My heart pounded, and my hands were clammy with sweat. Beads of perspiration trickled between my breasts, and the back of my cotton T-shirt clung to my skin.

I swung my free arm at him and screamed, "Stop it!" My hit wasn't hard, but it seemed to take him off guard. He let go and started to say something, but I didn't stick around to hear it. The strip mall was set into the foot of a wooded hill that stretched back for a quarter mile and was bordered on the other side by a country road. I ran away from him and up the hill. My thought was that I'd circle the building and try the back door to the dry cleaner's.

Under normal circumstances I could have outrun him, but the ground was slippery from the morning dew and I was out of breath. I couldn't go very fast. He lumbered behind me without breaking stride, and I felt him getting closer. When he reached out and struck my shoulder, I changed direction and went up the hill. Immediately I knew it was a bad move. There was no help up there. The property was mostly used by kids selling drugs. Every now and then the Girl Scouts used the site for nature walks, but no one would be there during summer vacation. We were almost at the top when he lunged forward and grabbed me around the waist. He was saying I shouldn't be afraid, that he wasn't going to hurt me, which is what all killers say on the crime shows on TV. He lifted me off my feet, and I yelled, "No, no, no."

He headed back down the hill with me pressed against him. Somehow I got a surge of strength. I swung my legs and slammed them against him, throwing him off balance.

When his grip loosened, I wiggled out of his grasp. Frantic, I tried making my way down the hill, but my Nikes slipped on the matted, slimy leaves and he was able to grab my arm. He squeezed it so tight I thought he'd break it. I pulled as hard as I could, but he held on.

I found my voice but couldn't speak above a whisper. I heard myself gasping, "Please, please, please," over and over again, not sure if I was pleading or praying. I had visions of someone finding me long afterwards—some kids smoking pot, or a group of Brownies stumbling upon my partially decomposed body on the rocky hillside.

"Come with me," he said, his face expressionless. "I want to show you something."

"Stop it. You're scaring me," I cried.

He let go then, and I toppled back, hitting the ground. The force of it made my heart rattle. I found myself rolling down the hill, the way we did on purpose when we were little kids, but this wasn't fun. As I tumbled over and over again, my face and arms smashed against the hard ground. I kept trying to get up, but I couldn't get a toehold. When I looked up, I saw him coming down the hill after me, and the sight gave me the strength to rise to my feet.

I scrambled down the incline and tripped over a tree root. As I fell I saw the large rock sticking out of the ground but couldn't react fast enough. When my head smashed against it, I swear I felt my brain explode inside of my skull. I was flat on my back and dazed when he caught up to me. Kneeling by my side, he lifted my head until our noses touched. I prayed faster and harder than I ever had before. I told God I was sorry for every bad thing I'd ever done, and I begged for my life. I wasn't ready to die. I reached up to push my attacker away, but he was too powerful and my hands weren't working right. He moved my head by cupping my chin, and then he pulled away and looked into my eyes. For a moment I thought he was going to kiss me. I said, "Please, no," my voice raspy and soft, and then everything went black.

Chapter 2

Initially my eyes refused to focus, so it took a while to make sense of where I was. The room was blurry and bright. The glare intensified the pain in my head. My grandmother sat to my right, her head bowed over a book. I recognized her as much by her floral perfume as by sight. For reasons I couldn't fathom, one of my eyes didn't want to open all the way, and my body felt heavy. The room was quiet except for the squeak of Grandma shifting in her chair.

I watched Grandma for what could have been minutes or hours. It was hard to tell. My eyes played tricks on me. She came in and out of focus like adjusting a manual lens camera. The lid of my left eye was heavy, so I watched mostly with my right. She sighed and turned a page, and I thought how familiar a sight that was, like seeing my own face in the mirror each morning when I brushed my teeth.

Grandma continued reading her book, but I could tell her heart wasn't in it. She glanced up for a moment and was startled by my one huge eye spying on her. "You're awake!" Her joy was unmistakable. "Oh, thank God, Angie." She dropped the book, and her hand went to her mouth as she rose out of the chair. She patted my cheek, and I flinched, every nerve ending in my body recoiling at the touch.

My lips moved, but nothing came out.

"Don't try to talk," she said. "I'll call the nurse." She reached over my body and fidgeted with something out of my range of vision.

I was in a hospital.

"Oh please," Grandma said impatiently, "they're not answering." She stood up and looked toward the door. "Stay right here; I'm going down to the nurses' station."

She was no sooner out the door than I heard a female voice coming from an intercom above my head. "Yes? You called?" I attempted to talk, but my throat was dry and the words wouldn't come. "Hello?" the same voice said. There was some talking in the background, and then the sound cut off and I was alone again.

I heard footsteps and my grandmother's voice as she came back down the hall toward my room. "Just five seconds ago," she said. "Her eyes are open. She recognized me, I know she did." Grandma entered the room first, followed by a woman in scrubs.

"Well there you are, Angie." The woman, a nurse I assumed, looked down at me. "How are you feeling?"

I was feeling beyond terrible, if she wanted to know the truth. Physically I ached from my heels to my scalp. I managed to move my head slightly and mouth an "Okay."

"You're at Trinity Hospital," she said, as if I had asked. "It's Monday, June tenth. You're safe here. We're going to take good care of you."

"Angie, do you know what happened?" My grandmother's voice rose in pitch. "Do you remember being attacked?" Her face above me wavered hazily, as if I were viewing it through water.

I opened my mouth, but despite my best efforts, I couldn't make the sounds into words.

"What, honey?" Grandma said. And then she asked the nurse, "What did she say? Did you catch that?"

"Hush," the nurse said soothingly to me, ignoring her question. "It's okay not to talk. Take your time." She leaned over me and grasped my hands in hers. "Can you squeeze my fingers? Good. Now squeeze harder." Pressing on her hands required as much effort as lifting a heavy grocery bag. "Now just the right." I hesitated. "This one is your right," she said, giving my fingers a gentle tap. "Good. Now your left." I concentrated and did exactly what she wanted. "Now see if you can focus on my finger." She moved her finger slowly from side to side and then from my forehead to my chin. I willed my eyes to follow. "Very good."

"That means she's going to be fine, doesn't it?" my grandmother asked.

"She's responsive. Always a positive sign."

"They said she might not remember anything. Do you think she remembers? The police want to question her."

"It's hard to say at this point. I'm going to page the doctor." The nurse's shoes on the linoleum made a swooshing sound as she exited the room.

"You've been here two days," Grandma said, stroking my hair like she did when I was ill as a child. "I've been sitting here waiting and praying." Her voice broke to a whisper. "I was afraid I was going to lose you too..."

Chapter 3

I was groggy for a long time after regaining consciousness. A stream of doctors and nurses came in and out of my hospital room, checking my eyes with tiny flashlights, asking questions, having me squeeze hands, instructing me to move my limbs. You'd think with all their modern technology they'd have more than that to go on. Later they inserted me into a cylindrical coffin of sorts, my head strapped with Velcro to hold it steady, the sound of drums reverberating all around me—an MRI, I realized later, but at the time I was too out of it to know or care. Things just happened to me. People talked soothingly, but I didn't always understand what they were saying. For a few days there I lived a dog's life.

It turned out I had a lot of bruises, broken ribs, a sprained wrist, a swollen eye, and a hairline skull fracture. All the doctors said I would be fine.

Jason was the first one in the family to know I'd been attacked. The police called home and woke him out of a sound sleep. To figure out my identity, the cops had connected the dry cleaning receipt in my pants pocket with my wallet on the front seat of the unlocked Honda in the parking lot. Pretty good detective work for our small town.

Besides my grandmother, I had plenty of other visitors. There was Jason and Grandma's fiancé Arthur, and Aunt Carla and Uncle Bob. And a lot of my friends came and went, day in and day out. I was glad to see them all, but I wasn't very good company.

At first Grandma never left my side. She brought me water and read to me, made sure I was comfortable. Told people to leave when I got too tired to talk. Grandma and I were close, really close, not because of something we had in common, but because of what we were missing. One person. The most important person in the world to both of us—her daughter, my mother: Laura Favorite, a beautiful woman with dark hair and big brown eyes, gone.

On my eleventh birthday, my mother disappeared. That morning my mom drove Jason and me to school. When we arrived, she helped me carry in a large Tupperware container full of cupcakes, made small talk with my teacher, told me to have a good day, and kissed me good-bye.

I never saw her again.

When she didn't arrive to pick us up from school, Jason and I walked home, but she wasn't there either. My father, who was in the den playing his guitar at the time, had no clue as to where she could be. He made some phone calls, and when he explained the situation to Grandma, she stepped in and called the police. My mother's car was found in the parking lot of the dentist's office where she worked, but no one there had seen her that day. The police investigated and found nothing.

One day we had a mother, the next, we didn't. My grandfather had died unexpectedly the month before, so there was some speculation by the authorities that my mom had been depressed and took off, but that was quickly ruled out. My grandmother was adamant about that. "My daughter would never, *ever* leave her children, much less on Angie's birthday," she told the police.

"She adores these kids and feels the same way about her husband, that Elroy." He was always *that* Elroy. She didn't approve of him much. "Laura didn't just walk off. Something happened to her." Grandma spent years hiring private investigators and offering rewards, trying to get the word out, but nothing ever came of it, except that she went through most of her money and had to sell her house.

Not having a mother left a horrible hole in my life. I kept waiting for her to come back, like she'd just gone to the store and would be returning soon. The first few weeks after she disappeared, I sometimes went into my parents' bedroom and stood in among the clothes in her closet, just to get the feel and smell of her. Everyone said I was the spitting image of my mother, so I'd look in the mirror and study my dark eyes, straight brown hair, and thin nose, as if that would bring her back. A few months later, my dad was arrested on a bogus drug charge. One evening he was out driving with a buddy, and they were stopped for a busted taillight. The cop searched the car and found drugs under the front seat. The stuff belonged to his friend, but that didn't make a difference. After that happened, Jason and I and our cat Misty went to live with Grandma. With most of my mother's things packed away, I didn't have daily reminders, but her absence was always with me.

I lost my mom, my dad, and my home in a few short months. We were a fractured family—separated, missing, lost. And we never reconnected. Even after Dad got out of prison we stayed with Grandma, who was by then our legal guardian. Living with her was the best thing, she said, since my dad was always traveling with his band. He got frequent visitation, like we were part of a divorce. Later he said he agreed so that we'd have a stable home life. Plus, he always believed it was only a matter of time before he'd make it big with his music, and then things would change and the three of us would be together again. He was always on the cusp of great success, or so he thought. Dad told us stories of record deals in the makings and managers who were interested in taking the band to the "next level." Once that happened, he said, he'd buy a big house and plan his touring around our school schedule. And we'd never have to worry about money again. That was his plan, and it was a good one, but it never came to be. In the meantime, he did the best he could. He came around as often as possible and called when he was on the road. My friends thought it was cool to have a rocker dad, but I would have preferred a regular family.

I missed my mom so much. Most kids loved their birthday, but mine made me cry every time. I used to feel like my birthday was responsible for her going missing. Would things have been different if she hadn't stopped to drop off the cupcakes? I always wondered.

I thought about my mother a lot, and I mean *a lot,* like constantly, but Jason didn't obsess like I did. "Do you ever think about her?" I asked once when I was working on a family history my freshman year.

"Sometimes, but I try not to," he said. "Dwelling on it won't bring her back." He, like most everyone else, believed she was dead.

I knew it wasn't true. Every night I prayed for her to be returned to us. And sometimes, I felt her praying the same thing back.

My second waking day at the hospital, my grandmother filled in the missing pieces between my ordeal on the hillside and my arrival at the hospital. No one could understand why I'd left my car since the dress, still in its dry-cleaning bag, hung in the backseat. Grandma told me later that the detectives speculated that the wallet in the front seat meant I'd been dragged out of the vehicle.

At some point two detectives came in to question me: a man in a dark-colored business suit and a young woman in uniform. The man was hefty, carrying the bulk of his weight around his middle, like a kid at the beach with an inner tube around his waist. I couldn't imagine him running through back alleys after a suspect or restraining a guy at a bar fight. Still, the way he scribbled earnestly in a small notebook gave him credibility. The woman cop didn't speak much; in fact, she seemed to have trouble even looking in my direction. I noticed her wince at first sight of my bruised face.

I was embarrassed to tell them I'd deliberately left the wallet in the car. They exchanged a glance like they thought I was a complete idiot. Somehow, the story of the quick run back to return the extra change lost something in the retelling. The detective asked numerous questions about my attacker. I told them what I remembered, but it didn't seem to satisfy them.

"Is there anything else you can remember?" my grandmother asked. She sat on the edge of the bed and held my left hand. "Maybe he said something that would explain why he picked you?" She stroked my knuckles encouragingly.

"I don't know," I said, but my words didn't fully convey my thoughts on the subject. Why he picked me? This wasn't an Internet dating service. He attacked me in a deserted parking lot. Her wording made it sound like I shared part of the blame. The two detectives standing at the foot of the bed were silent except for the scratching of pen against paper.

"We'll be in touch," the woman said, handing my grand-mother a business card. She gave me one last concerned look. "If you think of anything else, give us a call."

After they left, Grandma went into fuss mode—straighten-ing my blankets and smoothing my hair away from my face. When I said I wanted a sip of water, she adjusted the bed so I was partially sitting up and then held the cup under my chin.

"I've got it," I said, grasping the white Styrofoam cup with both hands. It took me three tries to get the end of the straw to my lips. I rested the cup on my stomach and closed my eyes. "Do you think they'll be able to find the guy?" I asked.

"Find the guy?" She took the cup out of my hands. I heard her set it on the freestanding tray next to my bed. "What guy?"

"The one who did this," I said, motioning to my banged-up cheeks with a limp wave of my fingertips. She didn't answer right away. I thought at first that she didn't hear me. When I opened my eyes, I saw an odd look cross her face.

"Oh honey," she said, dismayed. "They did catch him. Don't you remember?" She reached over and ran a fingertip slowly up and down my arm. The sensation gave me goose bumps.

The room was quiet while I tried to figure out what she was talking about. The door to the hallway was slightly ajar. Outside a petite woman in powder-blue scrubs pushed a cart with one of those squeaky, uncooperative wheels that spins in circles.

"How could I remember?" I said at last. "I was unconscious."

"I thought you knew," she said with a sigh, and then she proceeded to fill me in. I clutched the edge of the blanket and let her words wash over me. Even though this had happened to me just days before, I had the sense I was listening to someone else's life or hearing the plotline of a movie of the week.

The hillside hadn't been completely deserted after all. Two girls from my high school, a year older than me like Jason, were in the woods waiting for a friend when they saw my attacker dragging me up the hillside. These two girls figured out the situation right away, and one of them whipped out her cell phone and dialed 911.

"They did some quick thinking," Grandma said cheerfully. "One of them walked down to the parking lot to guide the police, and the other one stayed hidden nearby on the phone."

"They didn't try to help me?"

"Well, honey, they did help you. They were following the 911 operator's instructions, which was to stay out of sight. The police said they did the right thing. They're heroes, actually," she said. "Everyone's talking about it. They were interviewed by all the local news stations."

I digested this information. It was hard to hear that other people were nearby and did nothing to help. "Who were they?" I asked finally. "The girls who called 911—what were their names?" As much as I wished they had come to my rescue, I had to admit they might have saved my life.

"Lauren and Kelsey. Nice girls." She nodded in my direction. "Amazing really, the way they just happened to be in the right place at the right time. If it weren't for them, you could have died. The newspaper said they were like your own personal guardian angels."

Now that was a scary thought: two teenagers who were probably waiting for their dealer were all that had stood between death and me.

I found out more about my saviors when Jason brought the newspaper article about my attack and rescue. He read the article aloud in his best anchorman voice, accompanied by sound effects and grimaces. "Local Girl Saved," my brother boomed, with the emphasis on the word *saved*. He set the paper down and raised his hands in the air like he was singing the "Hallelujah Chorus."

"Okay, enough with the theatrics," I said.

"But the theatrics are what makes it fun." He picked up the newspaper and continued word by torturous word. "Witnesses to the crime, Lauren Buck and Kelsey Krautkramer..." He halted for commentary. "Get a load of those names—Buck and Krautkramer. What's the story there?"

"With a last name like Favorite, you should talk."

"Favorite's a cool name," Jason said with absolute certainty.

"Says who?"

"Dad."

No arguing with that one. Coolness was Dad's one strength. I asked, "Do you know those girls?"

Jason shrugged. "I know who they are, but we don't exactly run in the same circles, if you know what I mean."

Being immobile in a hospital bed gave me a chance to look at my brother sitting still. In the apartment he was usually in his room. We got along okay, and he could be a lot of fun when he wanted to be, but most of the time he just liked to be on his own. He played one of those geeky online games with the mutating fighting creatures. The other people he played against were from all over the world. I heard him talking to them through his headset.

Jason looked like a younger version of our dad: thick, dark hair, ink-black eyes, and tall, really tall. But Dad was a musician and lived to perform to a crowd, the complete opposite of my brother. Jason didn't mind other people, he just didn't *need* them. All he needed were books and a computer. He was a brain.

Grandma never allowed him to skip a grade. Dad always wanted him to—his son the genius skipping up the academic ladder with the greatest of ease, like a seal doing tricks in the circus. But my grandmother thought it would set him apart from the other kids, and besides, what was the big hurry?

This past year, his junior year, they compromised. Jason spent mornings at the high school and afternoons taking college courses at the university. Since Jason never got his driver's license, Dad drove him. When Dad was out of town, Jason took the bus. Driving together gave my dad and brother some common ground. Spending time together had gotten to be a problem for them. Jason had no interest in learning how to shoot pool or play the guitar, and Dad didn't have much interest in anything else. In the car they gained a new appreciation for each other. Dad once told me, with pride, "He's so smart, half the time I don't even know what the hell he's talking about." Tell me about it.

Jason still didn't have his driver's license. Everyone thought it was because he just wasn't interested; that's what he told them, anyway. I heard Grandma say, "Just give him time. Boys mature more slowly than girls." What she didn't know was that he held back on purpose to save her money. Someone had told him what insurance for a guy his age cost, and he didn't want her to have to pay it. He was like that a lot—doing nice things but not wanting to make a big deal out of it.

While I lay there looking at Jason, he was still reading. Hearing him describe the attack was painful. Mentally I pressed the mute button on Jason's words and was dozing off when I realized he was asking me a question.

"What?" I asked, jarred.

"Is that true?"

"Is what true?"

He held the newspaper up in the air and pointed, as if that would help me understand. "It says you're expected to be released from the hospital Thursday and will be convalescing at the home of relatives."

I searched my memory for an answer. Finally I said, "I don't think so. Not that anyone's told me."

Jason folded the newspaper carefully and set it on his lap. "If you're getting released from the hospital so soon," he said slowly, "that explains why Grandma and Uncle Bob keep talking about where you're going to go. They're all worried about it."

"They are?"

"Sure, they talk about it constantly. They don't think I hear them, but I do."

I knew Arthur and Grandma had a Caribbean cruise planned—their honeymoon, which was kind of a sweet concept considering they were way beyond the honeymoon age. She'd been talking lately about how they could put off the wedding, but not the trip. The tickets were nonrefundable and nontransferable. I couldn't remember, though, if she'd actually told me they were going.

The original plan was that Jason and I were going to stay with friends for the two weeks Grandma and her new husband were gone. It had all been arranged with my friend Shawnee's parents. No problem, they'd said. Now I was guessing they didn't want a messed-up, recently released hospital girl as a guest.

Staying with Aunt Carla and Uncle Bob was not something I wanted to do. Uncle Bob was our mother's brother. He was okay. It was his wife who was the problem. She hated us in that pretending-to-love-them-but-really-hating-them kind of way. I could imagine that having us at their house would be an infringement on her busy schedule of tennis, spa appointments, and sessions with her personal trainer at the club. She even made answering the phone sound like a huge imposition. "No, Angie," she'd say briskly, "Bob's not here. I'll tell him you called. Buh-bye." And then click, back she went to the other line, presumably to talk to someone more important than me.

Bob idolized Carla, proof positive that love was blind.

"Grandma says staying at Carla and Bob's would be best, but Uncle Bob says Aunt Carla's not happy about it," Jason said. "You know how she can be."

"Why can't we just stay home by ourselves?" I asked Jason.

He snorted. "Yeah, like that's going to happen. Grandma wouldn't have let us do that when you were well, and now that you're injured there's no way."

"Maybe Dad could stay with us." He would have to move in at Grandma's since his place was a one-bedroom apartment above a bar.

"That would never work. Grandma wouldn't allow it. Plus he's on the road right now, and I haven't been able to get a hold of him on his cell. I left a message on his voice mail, but I haven't heard back from him yet."

He said it like I wouldn't remember that Dad wasn't around. Of course I knew that he was on tour and hadn't come to see me; in fact, he didn't even know I'd been attacked since no one could reach him. Grandma had mentioned it several times, muttering under her breath about how irresponsible he was. But she didn't understand about the tour and how it was his band's last shot at making it big time. They'd finally landed a manager with great connections, and all of them were hoping this was it. Personally, I thought they were a little old for that. My take on it was that if it was going to happen, it would have already. Still, good luck and all that. He had a big heart, my dad, but he was kind of a mess at times.

"So where am I going to go?" I asked the question aloud, though I was mostly thinking to myself.

"The last I heard, you're going to Uncle Bob's, and I'll stay at Ralph's."

"What? No!" I had a sudden sick feeling in my stomach that had nothing to do with my injuries or any medications. I blinked back tears. There was no way I wanted to stay with Uncle Bob and his wife Carla. I had a hard enough time *visiting* them. Staying in Carla's house would be torture.

"I'm just telling you what I heard." Jason reached out and uncharacteristically patted my arm. "It would only be for a little while, Angie. I can visit you every day."

"Oh no," I wailed. I felt a big tear well up in my good eye. It lingered for a moment, distorting my vision like a strong lens. I blinked it away.

"Don't cry, Ange. I hate it when you cry." He brushed a lock of hair out of his eyes and squeezed my hand, his skin warm against my cold fingertips. He never would have held my hand under normal circumstances. The fact that he was doing it now meant I was totally screwed.

Chapter 4

Someone stroked my hair while I dozed. "Hey," I said, struggling toward wakefulness.

"Oh Angel girl," Dad said. I heard the scrape of a chair against the linoleum. When I opened my eyes, he was standing over me, staring intently. "You look terrible. You poor baby." He leaned forward and kissed my cheek. "Does it still hurt?"

"Kind of." I was so glad to see him. "Not as bad as before."

"I came as soon as I heard. I would have been here sooner, but my cell phone wasn't working because I forgot to bring my charger. I finally got your brother's message, and I got on the next plane."

He frowned and ran a hand through his thick, black hair. "I can't believe someone did this to you. Jason said you looked awful, but he didn't say you were purple and green."

My bruises. Without a mirror nearby, I tended to forget about them. "Actually, they've faded a lot."

"So you're saying it was worse before? God Almighty." His loud voice was a welcome change from the soft-spoken, patronizing tones of the hospital staff and my other visitors. He settled back in the chair and rested his feet on the edge of the bed, one cowboy boot crossed over the other.

"I'm getting better, though," I said. "The doctors expect a full recovery."

"Yeah, well." With most people, conversations were made up of words. With Dad you had to read the silences as well. His song lyrics gave me more clues about who he was than any discussion we'd ever had. "It just about killed me when I heard. I feel terrible that I didn't have my phone charged." He cleared his throat. "You know it's funny, but even before I listened to Jason's message, I just knew something bad had happened. I had one of those feelings I get." He looked like he might cry.

I nodded. His psychic hunches again. Really accurate, but again, not so great with the timing. He studied my face as if the bruises were a road map. Neither of us spoke for a few minutes.

"If you don't want those," he said finally, motioning to something on the table next to my bed, "I'll eat 'em." He had a big grin on his face. I could see the one front tooth that slightly overlapped its neighbor.

"What?" I asked, confused.

"The pistachios," he said and picked up the bag to show me.

My heart melted at the sight. "Pistachios. My favorite." Dad was the only one who ever bought me pistachios. No one else liked them as much as we did. When we got on a roll, my dad and I could go through a bag in no time at all.

Dad pulled a wastebasket from the other side of the bed and positioned it on the floor between us. I watched as he spread a tissue on the freestanding tray next to my bed and methodically cracked nuts. Down the hall came the sounds of a woman crying out in pain followed by rapid footsteps, but here in my room it was peaceful. The sight of my father sorting nuts on the tissue, throwing shells in the wastebasket, was oddly comforting.

When he'd amassed a small pile, I felt compelled to speak. "Are you ever going to let me have some?"

"Patience, young Jedi." He grinned and held a piece in front of my face. "They're coming your way. Just open up." Obediently I opened my mouth and let him drop it onto my tongue. He popped one into his mouth as well. The crunching of our chewing was the only sound in the room.

After a while he said, "I've got good news for you, Angie. I talked your grandma into letting me stay with you and Jason while she's on her cruise."

What a relief. "How'd you manage that?"

"She ran out of options. You know she had to be really desperate to let me sleep at her place." So true. My parents had been high-school sweethearts, and Grandma disliked him from day one. For some reason, it had bothered my grandmother that my dad drove a retired black hearse he'd bought from Mortenson's Funeral Home. Dad had told me it looked the same as when it transported the dead, with the exception of the red flames he'd painted on the side.

When I was about ten, I'd asked my mom how she and my dad met, and her eyes lit up at the memory. He was like the rock star in their high school, she said. The other kids treated him like a visiting dignitary, clustering around him in the hallways, clapping him on the back, listening to his jokes.

My dad grew up in a little farmhouse on the highway at the edge of town. He once told me that when he was a teenager you could drive by their house any time of the day or night and find the garage lit up, the sounds of power tools or rock music blaring from within. Dad was one of four boys, and they were wild. They drank beer and skipped school and violated curfew. They were known as the white-trash family from the wrong side of the tracks. My mother, on the other hand, was a nice girl and a good student. She said she wore nerd glasses and worried constantly about grades and fitting in. Then she met my dad, and she stopped worrying. They were mismatched, but so in love. In the early days Mom sang in Dad's rock band, but once they had Jason and me, the only singing she did was around the house and at church. I would have loved to have inherited her beautiful voice, but it must have skipped a generation because I can't sing in tune to save my soul.

Academically, Dad just squeaked by. Mom said that in speech class he stood at the podium and winged a talk so entertainingly the teacher had to give him a passing grade even though he hadn't done any research or turned in the note cards. In biology, he brought in live crayfish and lobsters during the exoskeleton unit. In home ec, he cooked them. He got extra credit for both. To fill the gaps of those subjects not conducive to props, he relied on hangers-on to help him out, either by copying off their tests or conning them into writing papers for him. When they first starting dating at Christmastime of his senior year, it looked like Dad would be the first Favorite to graduate from high school.

The rest of the story I heard from my father years later. Apparently the only thing more shocking than Dad actually graduating was the fact that my mom was six months pregnant with Jason when she crossed the stage to get their diplomas. My grandma said he ruined her life, but I wasn't so sure about that. We were a happy family. I still remembered how they laughed almost every single day.

After Mom disappeared, Grandma couldn't stand the sight of my dad; it was as if she blamed him. I wished she could hear the way he talked about Mom to us kids. He adored her and never took off his wedding ring. His dresser was practically a shrine to her, with photos and some of her favorite things—shells and jewelry and greeting cards he'd saved. They were still legally married, and as far as I knew, Dad wasn't looking elsewhere.

"Well, it's good that you're staying with us," I told Dad. "I was really worried about where I was going to go."

"I got you covered," he said. "You want to hear something else kind of weird? A long time ago, I knew the brother of the guy who attacked you."

"What?" I was having trouble following for some reason.

"Scott Bittner, the guy who beat you up? His brother used to hang with your Uncle Dino in high school."

"That's so weird."

"Yeah, kind of a freaky coincidence. Uncle Dino said he was going to kill Scott Bittner when he got out of jail, and I said not if I got to him first." Dad's face turned serious.

"Don't even talk like that," I said. "I don't want you to go to jail." I didn't add the word "again" although I could have. Dad's five months in prison was a sore subject. He'd said the drugs they found in his car weren't his, and I believed him. He ran with a pretty bad crowd when he was younger, but now all he had was an occasional beer.

Dad said, "Dino said Scott has a lot of mental problems and was always away at special schools and in hospitals back then. I told him I didn't give a rat's ass about his mental problems. I'll kill him if he goes near my daughter again."

"I don't want to deal with this right now." I closed my eyes. Up until then, I'd avoided thinking about my attacker, but at that moment the memories came flooding back. I could feel his arms squeezing my ribcage and smell his rank breath on my face. I remembered scrabbling over the hillside, frantic to get away. At the memory my heart started pounding like it had in

Karen McQuestion

the woods, and I couldn't catch my breath. My heart thumped harder and louder, and I felt like someone was sitting on my chest. "I think I'm having a heart attack," I gasped.

"I'll get the nurse," he said, in a panic, and was out the door before I could even point to the call button next to my bed.

I was dying, I was sure of it. Nobody could have their heart beat that fast and survive. Beating wasn't even the right word—it was more like pounding, drumming, slamming, like it wanted to escape my chest.

Dad pulled a nurse into the room by her arm. "It's going to be okay, I'm here," the nurse said as she stood by my bed. The fact that she would be present for my death wasn't reassuring to me at all.

The ID badge that hung around her neck identified her as Bridget. I tried to tell Bridget I was dying, but she grasped my hands and took over. "No talking," she said. "Deep, slow breaths." She demonstrated, as if I didn't know how to inhale and exhale like a normal person. Like I was gasping for the hell of it. Couldn't she understand how serious this was? Why wasn't anyone calling a code and running in with that cart with the electric paddles? Left on its own, my body was going to short out.

"Deep, slow breaths," she repeated sternly, and then she demonstrated again.

Somehow I managed to get hold of some air and then exhale at a more regular rate. "Keep going," she said, "like this." She sucked in air until her cheeks dented and then slowly let it out again. She leaned over and placed a stethoscope on my heart. I felt the coolness of the metal through my cotton nightgown.

"You said she was very upset when this started?" the nurse asked my dad, who stood next to her, stricken.

28

He nodded. "We were talking about the guy who attacked her."

Bridget held the stethoscope against me. I could feel the pressure of her fingertips against the rim of the metal. "Atta girl," she said to me. "You're doing fine. Keep that breathing steady. Your heart rate is coming down."

"What's wrong with her?"

"I think she's having an anxiety attack," Bridget said. "It's unlikely to be an actual problem with her heart, but the other nurse is getting the doctor. Just to be on the safe side, we'll get an EKG. We don't take any chances."

"Why would she be having an anxiety attack now?" Dad sounded bewildered.

"It's not that uncommon under the circumstances. A person doesn't go through what Angie did and just go on with their life. There's usually some sort of aftermath. The nurses have been watching for it." She directed the next comment to me. "It's okay. This is a good thing."

It didn't feel like a good thing.

She lifted the end of the stethoscope off my chest. "Sometimes crime victims go through the signs of grief, the way people do when there's been a death. Anger is the most common. Sometimes they become anxious, can't shake the fear that something bad will happen to them again. Everyone is different, but only a very few people get back to how they were before without some kind of help." She shook her head as if this were a shame. "Your heart rate is slowing down nicely. When it happens again, you'll need to concentrate on your breathing."

When it happens again?

"You really should talk to a counselor," she said gently, resting a hand on my arm. "If you don't work through this, it will just stay with you." She stood over me for a few minutes. Her other hand rested lightly on my abdomen. The pressure reminded me to take long, deep breaths. At her side, Dad looked less worried and more antsy—he shifted from foot to foot.

"I really think there's a serious problem with my heart," I said. Even now my pulse raced, although it no longer felt out of control.

Bridget looked dubious but glanced in the direction of the hallway. "I'll go see what's keeping them. I'll only be a minute."

"I'll be with her," Dad said.

Two hours and many adhesive-attached electrodes on my chest later, the medical staff had ruled out a heart attack.

"Well," my dad said, "that was scary. I'm glad it's over."

"For now," I said.

Dad patted my arm. "If it makes you feel any better, this happened to me once too. Just like you, I was breathing real hard, my heart was going a mile a minute. I didn't know it was an anxiety attack, though. I just thought I was scared."

I raked my hand through my hair, which felt limp and in need of shampoo. I desperately wanted a regular shower. I could only imagine how much my legs needed shaving. "What were you scared of?"

"Dying, I guess. It was in an elevator."

"When was this?"

"A couple months ago. The guys and I were playing a gig in this ratty old hotel in Kenosha. We were playing on the fifth floor—the ballroom. Well, it was called the ballroom, but it was a pit, one of those places where the toilet stalls don't even have doors on them, you know." I thought that probably described most of the places his band played. "We were taking this old freight elevator to haul all our equipment down after the show, and suddenly it gets stuck halfway between the floors. Then it starts shuddering like something's coming loose." To illustrate, he made his upper body shiver. "Shorty had a few beers, so he starts laughing and cracking jokes. All the rest of the guys are banging on the door and yelling for help. But me, well, I just fell apart. My heart was banging, and everything was sort of swirling around, and suddenly I couldn't stand up anymore. I kind of slid down into a crouch and put my head between my knees. I closed my eyes and just prayed for it to be over."

"I never heard about this."

He shrugged. "Not much to tell. I stayed all freaked out down in the corner until one of the hotel guys heard us and yelled to hang on. They said it happened all the time. Can you believe that? The thing didn't even have an escape hatch, so they had to pry the door open with a crowbar. It was halfway between floors, so we had to crawl out the bottom and drop to the floor." He sighed heavily and then smiled.

Something about his expression made me suspicious. "You didn't just make this up, did you?"

His face fell. "No, I swear. It really happened. Why would I make it up?"

"To make me feel better."

"So do you feel better?"

Actually, I did.

Chapter 5

On Friday, I went home. Before I left, Bridget and one of the other nurses came to see me off. Both of them gave me a hug, and I actually got a little teary saying good-bye. They called me their "favorite" patient (ha ha!) and said that they liked the fact that I wasn't a complainer. Maybe this was just the line they gave everyone, but it made me feel good.

The very next day, life went on the way it should. For everyone else, anyway. My grandmother and Arthur flew off to their cruise ship, Jason went to his lawn-mowing job and spent a lot of time on the computer, and Dad played the guitar, when he wasn't asking if I needed anything. He was on the phone a lot with the guys in his band. They'd cancelled their gigs for the next two weeks, and he was doing some composing in the meantime.

My cat Misty was especially glad to have me home, but she didn't seem to understand my limitations. She jumped in my lap and flicked her tail in my face until I yelled for Dad to pour food in her bowl. I did get visits from Shawnee and Maria and some other friends, but I still got tired easily and my head hurt. I wasn't much fun. Going out was something I kept putting off. Staying inside seemed safer.

Phone calls and the mail became the high points of my day. It was like I was ninety years old. Grandma did this really sweet, lame thing—she mailed me a card before she left with a message saying how much she missed me and apologizing again for leaving. We'd been over this a hundred times, and I could tell she was torn between staying with me and going with Arthur, but I meant it when I said I didn't mind if she went. She deserved a little happiness after all the years of searching for my mother and raising Jason and me. I did miss her—a lot, actually—but it was just for two weeks, and it was kind of a nice change having Dad around.

Every day Dad brought me the mail and let me sort through it. I found myself reading all of it—even the bills, the catalogs, and the ads. I got a lot of cards. Most of them were from relatives and teachers from school, and even though they had the standard messages—*Get well soon! Feel better!*—I was touched they took the time to show they cared. When I read one from Miss Charlesworth, my fifth-grade teacher, I actually started crying. She'd written, "Angie, I've been out of town and only learned about your terrible ordeal just now. Words can't tell you how sorry I am. You were always one of my favorite students and stood out as being one of the brightest, most caring girls I'd ever met. I know you won't let this incident define or diminish you as a person. Warmest wishes for a speedy recovery, Margot Charlesworth."

I read her words over and over again until I couldn't see through the tears. Miss Charlesworth had been my teacher the year my mother went missing. It was a terrible time, but having Miss Charlesworth as a teacher helped. Twice that year I had started crying at school, and it was just terrible. Everyone turned to look at me, and even though I looked down at my desk, I could feel their stares and hear their whispering. I knew they were saying my mom had run off with another man—that was the rumor started by a mean girl named Rachel. The first time I cried, Miss Charlesworth let me leave to go to the bathroom. The second time she dismissed the whole class for an early recess and let me stay behind in the safety of her classroom. After the other kids trooped out of the room, she crouched down next to my desk and handed me a Kleenex. "I don't know what happened to your mom, Angie," she said, patting my back. "But I know she wouldn't leave you and your brother. I could tell she loved you very much." Her words were just what I needed to hear.

Five days into my return home from the hospital, we had a slow mail day. Dad handed me two things—Grandma's *Reader's Digest* magazine and a linen-colored envelope with an unfamiliar address embossed in gold on the back flap: *2068 Lake Helen View Drive*. I turned the envelope around to see my name and address handwritten on the front.

"Do we know anyone on Lake Helen View Drive?"

Dad shrugged. "I don't—that's the rich end of town. Maybe a friend of your grandma's?" He left the room without waiting for me to open it. Obviously the suspense wasn't killing him.

I ran my fingers over the return address, feeling the raised gold letters like a blind person reading braille. Why so fancy? It was odd, like a wedding invitation or something. Despite how pretty the envelope was, I had a flash of something ominous. My hands trembled as I opened the envelope and pulled out a letter. The precise, formal writing was the same as on the outside of the envelope.

Dear Angel,
Words cannot express how sorry I was to hear about the injuries my son Scott inflicted on you. I was horrified beyond belief to hear what he had done. If I could trade places with you, I would in a heartbeat.

I'm not making excuses for Scott, by any means, since there is no excuse for what he did, but I wanted you to know he's battled demons all his life. Deep down, he's not a bad person.

If there is anything I can do to ease your suffering, just name it. My home and heart are completely open to you.

Warmest regards,

Lillian Bittner

At the bottom of the page she'd written her phone number, underlined it twice, and added, *"Please feel free to call me anytime for any reason."*

I read her words over and over again. At first I wasn't sure how I felt, and then a surge of anger welled up from inside me. *Deep down, he's not a bad person?* Give me a break. Yes, because *good* people often try to abduct teenage girls. Was the woman in complete denial? Her son tried to force me to go with him to God knows where, and he would have gotten away with it if those girls hadn't been out on the hillside that morning. Because of Scott Bittner, my mind, body, and soul were all messed up. I ached everywhere, was still a mass of bruises, and couldn't concentrate well enough to read or follow the plot of a movie. I didn't have a boyfriend now, and this wasn't going to improve my chances. For the rest of my life people would think of me as the girl who got attacked and nearly killed the summer before junior year. Life would never be the same again.

I could still hear his voice in my head. *Come with me. You need to see something.* The thought of what that meant still made me shudder. I'd come so close to being killed. I knew I should be grateful for my second chance at life, but I wasn't quite there yet.

And now Mrs. Bittner wanted to know if there was anything she could do to ease my suffering. How about going back in time and not raising a homicidal son? Get a clue, lady. Scott Bittner was probably one of those kids who tortured the family pet and bullied smaller children. Meanwhile, his parents looked the other way, thinking it was a phase he'd grow out of.

Scott, really a good person, deep down.

Yes, I was pissed.

Please feel free to call me anytime for any reason. I turned on my cell phone and punched in Mrs. Bittner's number. I didn't even try to stop myself. I wanted to hear her voice. I wanted to tell her there was nothing she could do to ease my suffering. That her son had done plenty already.

A man answered. "Bittner residence."

I tightened my grip on the phone. "Yes, I'd like to speak to Mrs. Bittner, please."

"Lillian's not available. May I take a message?"

"Yes. I mean no," I said. "I'll try her later. When would be a good time?"

"Is this Angel Favorite?"

In a moment of panic, I hung up. Hung up and instantly regretted it. Oh why had I done that? It was like something a grade-schooler would have done. I was just so shocked when he said my name. How could he have known? It couldn't have been from caller ID because I'd called from my cell.

I guess it didn't matter because for whatever reason he'd guessed it was me, and now I'd gone and hung up on whoever the hell he was. He'd certainly relay the fact that I'd called. He'd also say that I'd panicked and hung up like a complete idiot. There was only one thing to do: damage control. I redialed.

"Hello?" This time the man's voice was a little more cautious.

"This is Angie Favorite. I'm sorry, but I think we got disconnected." The lie slipped out so smoothly that *I* almost believed it.

"Oh, disconnected." The sound of relief came through the earpiece. "Maybe it was me. I probably pressed something by mistake. I'm so very sorry."

He thought he'd hung up on *me*—that was good. "It's okay. I've done that myself," I said. "Listen, can you tell me when it would be a good time to reach Mrs. Bittner?"

He hesitated. "I'm not sure. Lillian's lying down right now—she's had a terrible shock. Her son Scott passed away." He paused. "I might as well tell you—he killed himself."

Chapter 6

"He killed himself?" I repeated incredulously.

"Last night. You didn't hear about it?"

I swallowed hard over the lump in my throat. "No."

"He hanged himself in his cell. I'm not sure how he managed it—they were supposed to have him on suicide watch."

"Really," I said and was immediately aware of how lame the word sounded. But the truth was, I didn't know what to say. Saying I was sorry would have been a lie.

So many times I thought about what I'd say to Scott Bittner when I saw him face to face. Usually I pictured it happening in the courtroom when they sentenced him to eighty years in prison. I wanted to tell him that I no longer felt safe unless other people were with me, that unexpected noises made me jump, that I had bad dreams every single night. And I had questions: *How could you do this? Why did you do this?* And finally, *Why me?*

The fact that he was dead meant I'd never get a chance to confront him. He'd never be tried in court, never serve time. How convenient for him. I wasn't sorry he was dead. The only regret I had about his death was the timing. If it had happened a month earlier, I'd still be a whole person living my old life.

"Last night, you said?" It was the best I could do to keep up my end of the conversation.

"Yes," he answered. "Lillian is beside herself. She never was good at handling things. Scott has been troubled for a long time, but still it's a shock for her."

"Oh." I still didn't know who I was talking to and couldn't think of a graceful way to ask.

"I'll be sure to tell her you called." Before I could tell him not to bother, he'd said good-bye and hung up.

Misty hopped into my lap and rubbed her head against my hand. She was a mixture of Siamese and something else, and the Siamese half was responsible for the way she continuously "talked," sometimes sounding like a small, whiny baby. Now she looked up at me and mewed in Misty-language that she was so, so sorry I was taking the long road through Sucksville. In appreciation, I scratched behind her ears and ran my fingers down the length of her little furry body. I was still angry, but there was something else there too: sadness. Nothing would ever be the same again. It felt good to let it all out. I didn't even bother wiping the tears away, just sobbed and stroked my cat until Dad heard me and came in to pull me into a big hug. "What's wrong, baby?" he asked.

My answer: "Everything." I handed him the letter and buried my head in his shoulder. He gave me a hug and let me cry.

Chapter 7

I couldn't shake the feeling that I was at the bottom of a dark hole and I wasn't going to get out of it. Ever. Okay, I know that's a little melodramatic, but that's how it felt. It was so unfair that I couldn't function the way I wanted to. Getting up in the morning was an effort, and talking on the phone for more than ten minutes was impossible. Reading, which I used to love, muddled my mind. Watching mindless television and sleeping seemed to use up all my energy. Even chewing made me tired. Dad started making me protein smoothies, which went down pretty well. I slept around the clock, but I always felt tired.

I overheard Dad and Jason talking about me. They wondered if I should go for counseling, or if I'd snap out of this on my own. Dad wanted to give me time. Jason was for psychiatric intervention. I couldn't imagine that talking to some guy would change things, so I said no when they suggested making an appointment.

One evening a few days after Scott Bittner died, Jason and Dad ambushed me at dinner. "So, Angie," Dad said, "are you up for going somewhere?"

The way he said it made me suspicious. "Where?"

"I had a chat with Mrs. Bittner this afternoon," he said, watching to see my reaction. "She wanted to talk to you, but you were sleeping."

"What does she want?"

"She invited us to her house so she can apologize in person."

I took another bite of my dinner. Dad had made some kind of casserole with cream of cheddar soup and grated Parmesan cheese, which pretty much drowned out the taste of the canned tuna. Not too bad. "I really don't see the point. What does she want from me?"

"I don't think she expects anything from you. She said she just feels terrible about the whole thing. She feels..." Here Dad stopped to think. "She feels responsible."

"Well, so sorry about that." I didn't even try to hide the sarcasm. "But if she thinks this is going to be a Lifetime movie where I forgive her and we both cry and hug and make our peace with the situation, she's got another thing coming."

Jason reached over and touched my arm. "Angie, no one thinks you need to be nice about this. Say what's on your mind if you want. We've just been worried about you and thought it might bring you closure."

"I'm not sure I need closure," I said. "I'm just really pissed off." Both of them looked at me with concerned faces. Now I felt pissed off *and* guilty that I was causing them worry. I sniffed. "I'm sure I'll just get past this on my own."

Dad said, "I wouldn't have even brought it up, except I'm having one of my really strong feelings about this. I just think it's something you gotta do for some reason."

My dad's psychic hunches weren't the most convincing argument for having me visit my dead attacker's mother. It was all too weird. I said, "I just don't know if I feel up to this."

"It's up to you, Angel girl," Dad said. "But I have a feeling about this, a major psychic feeling. I'm sensing that this visit could be life-changing for you. Think about it."

Chapter 8

I thought about it all that night and the next morning. Jason's words especially stuck with me. Now that Scott was dead, I'd never get the chance to face him and tell him what he'd done to me, but I could speak my mind to his mother. Maybe, just maybe, it would lift me out of my black pit of depression. Anything would be better than the way I felt right then.

The next evening we climbed into Dad's old station wagon and headed out. With other people, I'd felt self-conscious about my bruises, but now I was glad they hadn't completely faded. Let Mrs. Bittner see what her son had done to me.

I watched out the window as we left our side of town and headed down a winding country highway. Dad turned onto the frontage road when we reached the lake.

"You better slow down," Jason said, looking at the MapQuest directions. "It's coming up quick."

"I know, I know," Dad said, although judging from the abrupt turn he made, he *didn't* know. We would have gone right by it if not for Jason's reminder. We pulled onto a paved road and followed it up to a set of wrought iron gates. Someone must have been watching for us, because the gates swung open as we approached. As soon as the car stopped at the top of the circular drive, Jason looked out the window and said, "This place is like two or three times the size of our apartment building. It's incredible."

After getting out of the car, all of us paused to stare at the Bittner house. It looked like a castle. In fact, it was a castle, a solid gray structure with turrets and rounded windows. Even in the dusk of twilight I could see it was tall, maybe four or five stories if you counted the towers and turrets.

Enormous trees surrounded the house, the tallest branches blending into the evening sky. The front door was massive. If the owners lost their keys, they'd need a battering ram to force it open. On either side of the door, leaded-glass windows glowed from within.

Dad shook his head in wonder. "There's some serious money here, I tell you that much. Angie, I'm thinking my premonition might involve some kind of payoff. These people have plenty to spare. They could send some major cash our way and not even miss it." My dad was always wheeling and dealing, for all the good it did him.

A bald guy in a gray suit came out the front door and smiled. "Welcome to the Bittner home." My dad made the introductions, and the man identified himself as Hank; he said he'd worked for the Bittner family for thirty years. He ushered us into the house and immediately launched into a tour guide speech as we stood in the entryway. "Mrs. Bittner is so private that very few people ever visit here. Personally, I've always found the history of the house fascinating. It was built in the early nineteen hundreds, and it was the largest home on the lake at the time. Some of the best craftsmen in the world were brought in, and it took four years from beginning to completion."

Dad nodded while Jason and I stood nearby, me wondering why we were supposed to care.

Hank pointed down at his feet. "All of the tile in the home was imported from Italy."

Dad leaned over to get a closer look. "Impressive."

"And all the chandeliers in the house are made of Waterford crystal," Hank said, directing our attention upward.

The way he was showcasing the house was so weird, and I found myself getting annoyed. Didn't he know why we were there? "Is Mrs. Bittner here?" I said, aware that I sounded rude, but not caring. "If not, we can come back another time." I was starting to regret coming. Jason and Dad had said we could go the minute I wanted to leave. Knowing that helped.

"Oh, she's most definitely here," Hank said, leading us into a room that looked as if it hadn't been updated since—well, ever. Names like settee and divan and Chesterfield came to mind, even though I wasn't entirely sure what those words meant. Lamps on end tables had crystals dangling off the bottom of the glass-domed shades. The focal point of the room was a sitting area made up of an oval coffee table surrounded by a sofa and three chairs. "Mrs. Bittner knows you've arrived. She just needed a few moments to freshen up. Please make yourselves comfortable, and she'll be here shortly." He gestured for us to sit, and then he left the room.

I was starting to have a sick feeling that coming here was a very bad idea. "I'm not sure I can do this," I said, swallowing hard.

"Do you want to go?" Jason asked, sounding concerned, and then he turned to our father. "Dad, maybe we should go. She doesn't look very good."

Dad came over and put a hand on my shoulder. He leaned over and spoke into my ear. "What's wrong, Angie?"

"I have a *bad* feeling." One of those trapped, want-to-flee feelings.

"Like you're sick?" he asked.

"Not exactly, just like I don't want to be here."

Dad squeezed my shoulder. "We can go if you want to, Angie, but do you think we could we wait until we at least meet Mrs. Bittner? I wasn't going to mention this until later, but I Googled their family and they have this foundation thingy where they hand out money to deserving people. Scholarships and grants and stuff. I was thinking maybe—"

Mrs. Bittner appeared then, stopping in the doorway as if we were the ones who lived there and she was afraid to bother us. I'm not sure what I was expecting, but this woman wasn't it. For one, she didn't match what I remembered of her son. He'd been big and bulky and dark. She was prim and mousy. More of a librarian type than a rich society lady. "Hello," she said softly.

Jason stood up and said, "We're really sorry, but we need to leave. My sister doesn't feel good."

"Oh." She looked disappointed. "I'm sorry to hear that. Is there anything I can get you? Water? Hot tea, maybe?"

I said, "No thank you. I think I just need to get home and rest." I stood up, expecting she'd lead us out, but instead she walked toward me and put her fingertips under my chin—just for a second, before I even saw it coming. I flinched.

Mrs. Bittner lowered her arm and smiled. "Angie, I would have known you anywhere. You look so much like your mother."

I was shocked. People always said I resembled my mom, but I wasn't expecting that comment here. "Did you know her?" I asked.

She cleared her throat. "Well no, but I saw her photo in the paper, and also I remember seeing her around town with you and your brother before that." She pointed at me and wagged her finger. "It's uncanny how much you look like her. The spitting image. Such a beautiful lady, your mother, and such a lovely singing voice."

There was an awkward silence until my dad said, "Well, I guess we'll get going then. Sorry it didn't work out."

"Wait." It was me saying the word, but I wasn't sure where it came from. "It's okay. We can stay for a while."

"Are you sure?" Jason asked.

"Yeah, I feel a little better." Something made me want to stay. I wasn't sure what it was, but my dad wasn't the only one who believed in listening to that little voice inside.

Dad and I sat on the sofa, and Jason and Mrs. Bittner settled into the chairs. She smoothed the front of her pants and looked at each of us in turn as if trying to read our faces.

No one said a word. All of them seemed to be waiting for me to start the conversation. I took a deep breath and then exhaled before speaking to Mrs. Bittner. "I'm sorry for your loss." Someone had to say it. I wasn't sorry Scott was dead, but I wasn't completely heartless.

She gave me a sad smile. "That's very kind of you, especially with everything you've been through. When I heard what Scott did to you, I was sick. I couldn't sleep. I couldn't eat. I've been a wreck."

"I know the feeling," I said.

She looked upset. "I'm sorry, I didn't mean to downplay your troubles by telling you mine. If there's any way I can make it up to you, I will."

"I don't really think there's any way you can make it up to me," I said. "I mean, the damage is pretty much done. My head hurts, and I'm having trouble sleeping." I knew I was being mean, but I couldn't seem to stop myself. "Two of my ribs are broken, and my wrist is sprained." I held up the arm with the brace. "The worst of it is that I had a skull fracture." I left out the part about it being a hairline fracture. "Even after I heal, I'll never be the same."

Mrs. Bittner looked like I'd slapped her. "I know," she whispered. "I'm sorry." Now we both felt terrible, and I wasn't getting any closer to finding closure. This was the most messed-up meeting ever.

Dad leaned toward her. "Angie needed to get that out. You can understand where she's coming from."

She nodded, and there was a long pause. Jason cleared his throat, breaking the silence. "Did your sons grow up in this house?" He was pretty good with the social skills, when the occasion called for it.

"Yes," she said, smiling sadly, "both my boys grew up here, as did I." She told us her husband died when Scott was born and his brother Michael was six, so her sons grew up without a father. Both of her boys were a treat: helpful, kindhearted, good students. "Everyone thought so," she said emphatically. "Teachers, neighbors—everyone."

I wanted to tell her that I certainly hadn't found Scott to be a treat, that he wasn't helpful or kindhearted to me in the least. I was just about to say it when she beat me to it.

"Of course, that was before Scott showed signs of being so troubled. He was about eleven when it all started. At first his behavior wasn't too bad. He had learning disabilities and he got frustrated. Homework became a battle every night. Eventually he became more and more difficult, and I had to pull him out of school and have the teachers come here. No matter what I did, he only got worse. Sometimes he yelled so loud it frightened me. I tried everything—different drugs, different hospitals, different doctors, and finally, after his last stay the doctors said he was stable. He seemed fine. I thought I'd gotten my son back." She was interrupted by Hank entering the room carrying a large tray that held a tea set and dessert.

"Trudy's ill?" Mrs. Bittner asked.

Hank nodded and set down the teacups. "Trudy has a migraine, but she waited until the cake was done to take her medication. She's sleeping now. I'm sure she'll be fine."

Mrs. Bittner gave Hank a sympathetic look and then turned to us. "Hank and his wife have been working for my family for a long time. Trudy works as much as she can, but she's prone to headaches, poor thing."

Hank lifted the plates off the tray and set them in front of us—chocolate cake drizzled with fudge sauce and adorned with raspberries. I'd planned on turning down anything they offered, but both Dad and Jason were being polite and saying how delicious it looked, and I wasn't going to be the one to spoil things. So we sipped tea and ate cake like nice, civilized people. When we were finished, the timing would be right to leave. I was prepared to say I was tired. It was a good excuse, and true. Lately I was always tired.

"This is really good cake," Jason said, finishing off his piece ahead of the rest of us. He scraped his fork to get the residual crumbs and fudge sauce.

"Trudy's an excellent baker. And cook, too," Mrs. Bittner said. "I'm surprised we don't all weigh three hundred pounds."

"So there are three of you living here—you and Hank and Trudy?" Jason asked exactly what I'd been wondering.

Mrs. Bittner set down her teacup. "Not quite," she said. "Hank and Trudy live in the guesthouse." She sighed. "My in-laws moved in to help when my children were little, but they died a number of years ago. Scott was gone the last few years and just came home a month ago," she said. "My other son, Michael, hasn't lived here since he left for college. He and his wife have one child and own a home on the other side of the lake. Their son is named Michael too. Mikey, we call him. He's seventeen. He just graduated from high school and will be heading off to college at the end of August."

So she had a grandson only a year older than me, but two grades ahead of me. Mikey Bittner. He wouldn't have gone to my school, but I wondered if I'd ever seen him around.

When Hank came in to clear the plates, it seemed like time to call it a night. "I'm feeling a little tired," I said. "We probably should head for home."

"Oh please, let me show you the house before you go," Mrs. Bittner said. Without waiting for us to respond, she jumped up and led us out of the parlor and into a formal dining room that seated twenty. Mrs. Bittner said the crystal chandelier in the center of the room was an exact replica of one in the White House. I presumed she meant *the* White House, the one the president lived in. I wasn't about to let on that I was impressed, so I just nodded my head as if White House replicas were the norm with us too.

Every room was fancy like that. So much more than one family needed that it seemed like overkill. I thought of Grandma and how she'd worked her whole life and never known anything close to this lifestyle. How did the world get so crazy?

We wandered through smaller areas tucked in between the larger rooms. One part consisted entirely of glass cases holding plaques and trophies. Another contained two wing chairs with a knitting basket at the foot of one of them. The "knitting room," Mrs. Bittner called it.

The kitchen was fit for a gourmet chef, with an enormous glass-fronted cooler, two built-in ovens, and an enormous stove hooded by a copper awning. The kitchen table, set up with six chairs, seemed small by comparison. "This is where Trudy does her magic," Mrs. Bittner said when we entered. "We generally eat here." She pointed at the modest table. "When I was a child, my parents had elegant dinner parties, and the house was always filled with overnight guests. It hasn't been that way for a very long time."

When we found ourselves back in the entryway, Dad nodded toward the grand staircase and said, "That's a lot of stairs to climb."

"We have an elevator, so it's not a problem." She waved her hand, and we all stopped to look at the metal elevator doors. It looked a little out of place, like it had been added after the house was built, but I could see the advantage of it for such a big house.

"Now there's one more room you really must see." Mrs. Bittner led us down a hallway and stopped in front of a set of double doors. "The library," she said, opening the doors dramatically.

It was like something out of my dreams. The room was octagonally shaped with floor-to-ceiling bookcases and one of those sliding ladders to reach the upper shelves. A pair of over-sized leather chairs faced a tiled fireplace. The domed ceiling overhead reminded me of the rotunda in the state capitol building. Books of every shape and size occupied every inch of the shelves. Hundreds—no, thousands of volumes.

"Wow," I said, despite my intention to play it cool. "This is great."

"Angie loves to read," Dad said.

Mrs. Bittner beamed. "What do you like to read?" she asked.

"Everything," I answered, a vague reply but true. I loved thrillers, ghost stories, and stories set in different cultures. I liked reading about anyone who had an interesting life, from women who dressed up as men to fight in the Civil War, to the guy who invented Q-tips. If nothing else was available, I read junk mail and the backs of cereal boxes. Most recently Jason had turned me on to graphic novels. "Everything," I repeated and moved closer to the books so I could read the names on the spines. The room smelled faintly of lemon furniture polish.

"I thought you might be a reader," Mrs. Bittner said. "I used to be. I don't read much anymore, so the library doesn't get much use, I'm afraid. If you see anything you'd like to borrow, go ahead."

I could have taken any number of them home, but I didn't want her to feel like this would make everything okay. What Scott did couldn't be undone by a few books. I said, "No thank you. I'm having trouble concentrating lately. Because of my head injury."

Mrs. Bittner gave me a sympathetic look. "Well, maybe you might want to take a few anyway for when you feel better. You can keep them as long as you like. In fact," she added hastily, "you wouldn't have to return them at all. As you can see, we have so many."

We have so many. For some reason the words didn't sit right with me. I shook my head. "It's a nice offer, but I'm really not interested."

Mrs. Bittner wrung her hands. "Well, if you change your mind—"

"I think it's time to leave," I said. I was tired and was starting to get a headache. "I have to get up early for a doctor's appointment." Not true, but she didn't know that.

"We didn't get much of a chance to talk," Mrs. Bittner said.

"Sorry, but I'm not feeling very well."

"Of course. Maybe another time." Mrs. Bittner escorted us back down the hallway, through the knitting area, by the trophy cases and the dining room, and past a few other rooms I didn't remember seeing the first time through. By the time we reached the front door, I was starting to get that anxious feeling again.

"You okay, Angie?" Dad asked, noticing the look on my face.

"Yeah, I just need to go to bed, I think."

"Can I get you anything?" Mrs. Bittner asked.

"No thank you," I said. "We really have to go."

As we drove away from the Bittner castle, I had a nagging feeling about something that was said during our visit. I did a mental inventory. For one thing, Dad had never mentioned the Bittner Foundation money to Mrs. Bittner, which made me glad, but that wasn't what was bothering me. I thought about it all the way home, but it wasn't until we pulled into the parking lot of our apartment building that I figured it out. Mrs. Bittner had said she remembered my mother from her newspaper photo and from seeing her around town. The fact that she remembered was remarkable in itself, but she also said Mom had a lovely singing voice.

How would she know that?

Chapter 9

Two nights later I dreamt I was walking through the Bittner place. In the dream I was my old self, completely uninjured and free of pain. The house was dark, much darker than during our actual visit, and was lit only by candles. Mrs. Bittner was in the front hall, her hand raised in greeting, but I ignored her and walked by.

I wandered past the kitchen, where a woman I presumed to be Trudy stood at the table rolling out a piecrust, her lips pursed as if whistling. A bowl of peeled, sectioned apples sat on the table to her right. The front of her apron was covered with flour.

I saw Hank in a three-piece suit, standing next to the trophy case, a feather duster in hand. Like the human robots at Disney World, he turned his head slowly as I approached. "You don't want to go any farther," he said, raising his eyebrows. "You've seen too much already."

But despite a feeling of dread on my part, I did go on. I just had to. When I got to the library, I opened the double doors.

I walked in and the room was just as I remembered it, right down to the smell of wood polish and leather. The fireplace cast a glow from flickering flames. At first I thought the room was empty, but then I saw someone sitting in one of the oversized leather chairs facing the fireplace. From the doorway I could only see the back of a head. I moved closer, straining my neck to see. Bit by bit, step by step, I was almost there, and then—

"Angie, wake up." Jason's voice came through several layers of consciousness to reach me. I was aware of hands squeezing my shoulders. I wanted to stay in my dream world, but reality intruded and it all melted away.

I swatted at him like I would a pesky fly. "Stop it."

"Angie, you gotta wake up. Big news."

I grunted in response. Very few things in life are important enough to interrupt a good sleep. School, a job, a fire alarm—those things qualify, but that morning I was pretty sure none of those applied.

"Dad just got a phone call from the head of Preposterous Records. The guy loved their demo and wants to meet with them."

"What?" I opened my eyes and took a few moments to process this information. I was only halfway out of my dream tour of the Bittner castle. I could still hear the hiss of the fire. Jason's news seemed like it might be a continuation of the dream. "For real?"

"Yeah, for real. The people there liked their demo and want to meet the group. This could be their big break."

I was wide awake now and sitting up. "Tell me again." I rubbed my eyes.

"Dad and the guys are meeting with the top guy at Preposterous Records. He said they have a great commercial sound." Jason was smiling widely now, and I knew it was true.

"Really," I said. Dad always said this would happen someday, but I guess I didn't actually believe it would happen.

"The guy *loved* Dad's songs. Dad thinks that even if they don't sign the band, he might make some good connections for songwriting. There's some serious money there, if the right people want it."

"Unbelievable." This was unreal. If only Grandma were here—she'd be stunned. As long as Dad had been predicting his eventual success, my grandmother had been predicting his music would never amount to anything. And so far she'd been right. Much as I loved Grandma, I'd be happy for her to be wrong on this point. "Where's Dad now?"

"Calling all the guys. He wanted me to let you sleep, but I couldn't hold it in any longer. I just had to tell you."

I struggled out of bed to get to the kitchen and then settled into a chair. Dad, the phone against one ear, gave me a silly finger wave. He was grinning like I'd never seen him grin. So this was what it looked like when someone's dreams were coming true. Jason handed me a glass of orange juice and sat down next to me. When Dad finally hung up, I asked, "So, what's going on?"

He beamed, literally. I swear he was glowing. "Your old man is finally making it happen. LA, baby. I am so there." He ran his fingers through his hair. "Oh Angel, I said this would happen. Didn't I?"

"Yep, you did." I'd always thought this particular psychic hunch might just be wishful thinking on Dad's part, but here it was coming true.

"I saw it once, in a dream. It just took so long to happen; I was nearly ready to give up. But I didn't." He took a sip from his coffee mug. "The only one I haven't been able to get a hold of is Shorty. Man, he's gonna die when I tell him."

"When are you going?" Jason asked.

"We leave Thursday. And this is the best part: we're flying out and staying at a hotel there and the company's footing the bill. Meals and everything. Once I know all the guys are on board, I'm supposed to call the guy's assistant and she'll make the arrangements."

"How long will you be gone?" I said.

Dad's face fell. "That's the only bad part about this. We leave on Thursday, come back on Sunday."

Jason whistled. "That's one long meeting."

"It's not just one meeting. It's a lot of meetings with a lot of different people," he said. "Then, over the weekend, there's this show, and they're going to have a bunch of bands playing. He wants us to go and meet some people. They're pulling out all the stops for us." Jason and I exchanged a look. We were both thinking the same thing, which was that Dad had forgotten he was supposed to be staying with us. He could be flaky sometimes. But we were wrong, he hadn't forgotten, because the next thing he said was, "I figured you two could just stay here by yourselves. It's only three nights, and you *are* sixteen and seventeen. Good God, I was living on my own when I wasn't much older than you."

"Oh yeah!" Jason pumped his arm in the air. "I was worried you were going to make us stay with Uncle Bob or something."

"Nah, I wouldn't do that. Although if he calls, tell him I'm in the bathroom or something. Don't tell anyone I'm gone. Let's just keep this between the three of us. Your grandma would have a coronary if she knew I left you alone."

Chapter 10

I waited until Dad left town before calling all my friends to tell them Jason and I were on our own for a few days. Dad left us with a full fridge and two hundred dollars in twenties. I thought I'd invite some people over to watch a movie and have some pizza, but everyone already had plans for that night.

Shawnee was going to a movie with some Ryan guy, and even though she said she'd stop over on the weekend sometime, I could tell her heart wasn't in it. Maria was going to come and then cancelled at the last minute because her cousin got tickets to see a local band. I said they should come over beforehand, but that didn't work out for some reason. Some other friends had to work, and a few were on the class trip to Costa Rica. I hadn't been online much at all, and I'd forgotten about that. While some of my classmates were in Central America, my world had narrowed down to the walls of our apartment.

"*I'll* eat pizza with you," Jason said. He was only doing it to be nice, but it was better than eating alone.

I had the leftover pizza again the next morning. While I chewed, I realized that for the first time since I'd been home from the hospital I was bored. Really bored. Jason had left early to mow lawns, in the hopes of beating the rain, and wouldn't be back until later in the afternoon. I wasn't napping as much anymore. Instead, I took to lying on the couch, the remote in one hand. That's where I was when the phone rang that morning. Even though the caller ID said "Unknown Caller," which usually meant a telemarketer, I still answered it. That's how bored I was.

"Hello."

"Angie?" A woman's voice. "Is this Angie Favorite?"

"Yes, who is this?"

"It's Lillian Bittner. We met the other night."

"Oh yes." I fumbled with the remote and muted the sound. "How are you?" What could she possibly want?

"You came to my house?"

"Yes, I remember." There was a long pause before she cleared her throat like she was gearing up to say something. I waited for it, but there was only silence. I was getting impatient now. "Did we leave something behind?"

"No, nothing like that. I just so enjoyed meeting all of you, and I hoped we could get together again. I would love it if you'd come for dinner tonight."

"That's nice of you," I said, turning the sound back on, "but it really won't work out for tonight." There was a long pause— why wasn't she saying anything? "My dad is playing with his band, so he won't be home at dinnertime."

"I see. Well, maybe you and Jason could come out then? I could send Hank to pick you up, if you don't have a car."

Actually, I wasn't cleared to drive yet because of my head injury, but I wasn't going to tell her that. "No, thank you. I think we'll just take a pass."

"It wouldn't be any trouble at all. I'd love to have you."

"It's very nice of you to offer, but I've been pretty tired lately. I thought I'd just lay low for the rest of the day."

"Oh, are you sure? I was especially hoping tonight would work out because my grandson Mikey is going to be here." She sighed loudly. "Also, I wanted to discuss something with you and your brother. It's an opportunity for a full-ride college scholarship for both of you. It would cover tuition and books and living expenses at the university of your choice. You could get your degree essentially for free. This is through the Bittner Family Foundation, and I could arrange it all. Is that something that would interest you?"

"Maybe we could talk about that some other time," I said. "But thanks for calling." I clicked off then, more than a little irritated. The woman didn't pick up on social cues. When someone said they were busy, that meant *no* and you were supposed to let it drop. Everyone knew that.

When Jason got home, I gave him a play-by-play of my talk with Mrs. Bittner, ending with, "And then she says this scholarship through the Bittner Family Foundation would cover everything, so we could both go to college completely for free. Then she asked if this was something that would interest me."

"What did you say?"

"I told her we could talk some other time, and then I said good-bye."

"What?" He came closer and leaned in, his face just inches from mine. He had sweat stains under his arms, and I could smell the perspiration mixed with the scent of freshly cut grass. "You're kidding right?"

I gave him a gentle shove, and he took a step back. I said, "No, I'm not kidding. I told her we were busy, but she wouldn't let it go. Then she dangles this whole scholarship thing, like that's going to change everything. I kind of resent being bribed, if you must know."

"But if it's her family's foundation, it sounds like a sure thing..." He frowned. "I hope you didn't screw up our chances."

"Jason, don't get your hopes up. She can promise anything, but that doesn't mean it's going to happen. I definitely got the idea she was just throwing it out there to get us to come to dinner."

"But what if it's true? I mean, rich people are in their own league. Both of us get good grades, so we'd probably fit their guidelines. What if she can make it happen? Wouldn't that be great?" He raised his eyebrows and tilted his head to one side.

Sure it would be great, but even if it did happen, it would be guilt money. Did I want to be indebted to my attacker's mother?

"Maybe we *should* go for dinner," he continued. "What do we have to lose? Hank picks us up, we eat a good meal, you talk nice to the grandson, and maybe, just maybe, we both end up with full-ride scholarships."

"If we do get scholarships, it would only be because her son tried to kill me," I said. "It's blood money, Jason."

He shrugged. "Yeah, well so what? You've gone through hell. Why shouldn't you get something out of it?" I didn't have anything to say to that. "Come on, Angie." Now he was pleading. "Where's your spirit of adventure? We don't have anything else going on tonight. One dinner and we both might get a college education out of it. Say yes?"

"No."

"I'll be right with you the whole time. You don't even have to talk if you don't want to, just chew and smile. You don't even have to chew, just *pretend* to chew. Please?"

I sighed. He knew just how to get to me.

"Okay, you don't even have to smile if you don't want to," Jason said. "Just be there, and I'll handle the conversation end of things. Please? I'll never ask you to do anything again."

He was clearly not going to let this go. "Okay." I gave in reluctantly. "But you have to call her back and set it up because I'm not going to."

"Fair enough."

A nagging thought came to the surface, something I'd been meaning to ask my brother. "One more thing. Do you remember Mom singing?"

"Well, yeah. Of course. She was always singing."

"I don't just mean at home. Did she sing outside of the house?"

Jason gave me a puzzled look. "Like outdoors, you mean?"

"No, I mean like out in public," I said. "Where people besides family could hear her sing."

"In Dad's band, before we were born. After that, just at church, I guess."

The meter in my brain clicked an affirmative. Oh yes—church. Mom was in the choir and sometimes had solos. That's where Mrs. Bittner must have heard Mom sing. It all made sense now.

Chapter 11

It was overcast when Hank came to get us and drizzling by the time we arrived at the castle. He drove up in an ancient Cadillac Seville, a disappointment for my brother, who was hoping for a Rolls Royce or a stretch limo. The Caddy did have a smooth ride, I'll say that much for it. Jason rode in front with Hank, and they made small talk about road conditions and the thunderstorm we were supposed to get that night. Both of them agreed that a good rain was needed. It had been way too dry.

Hank drove up near the front door and had us wait while he opened a large umbrella and came around to our side of the car. "No need for you to get wet, Angie," he said after opening the car door and waiting for me to exit under the umbrella. And to my brother he said, "If you wait here, Jason, I'll be right back for you." Jason didn't listen, though, but followed right behind as we made our way to the entrance. It was only ten feet or so, and it wasn't raining that hard. Sticking around for the return of the umbrella would have been ridiculous.

Mrs. Bittner was waiting for us in the foyer. "Welcome, welcome," she said and then apologized for the rain, as if it had been her fault. True to his word, my brother handled things. He asked if we could see more of the house, and we got a tour of the second floor, including a ride in the elevator. It wheezed as it moved, and I swore I could hear the cables straining from the weight, but Mrs. Bittner didn't seem to notice, just kept talking about the house, things like who designed it and how it was built.

Most of the rooms on the second floor were bedrooms, all of them having their own distinct style. "Was this one of your sons' bedrooms?" Jason asked, peering into one with a nautical theme.

"Yes," she replied. "It was Michael's. It's always been a tradition in my family that family members had their bedrooms and study rooms on the second floor and that the third floor was reserved for guests. But that was way back when. We haven't used the third floor in ages. The only time anyone goes up there now is for spring cleaning."

An entire floor unused—it was a hard concept to wrap my rattled brain around. Whole families could live in this place. It seemed lonely for just one person. I felt a little bad for Mrs. Bittner, even if she was Scott's mother.

When we got back to the first floor, I was startled to see a guy my age sitting in a chair next to the grandfather clock. He was so engrossed in texting that he didn't even look up when the elevator doors slipped open. This had to be grandson Mikey. I was surprised to see he was normal looking and even kind of cute, if you liked the blond, shaggy-haired surfer type.

"Mikey!" Mrs. Bittner exclaimed.

He finished his message, snapped the phone shut, and stood up slowly. "I don't know why you sound so surprised, Grandma. You invited me."

"I know I invited you. But you don't always do what you're supposed to."

"I said I'd come." He tucked the phone into his pocket.

Mrs. Bittner grabbed his arm as if to keep him from wandering off. She introduced Jason and me as her honored guests.

"Call me Mike," he said and took my hand. He didn't really shake it, just held it and gave me a thorough looking over. "My grandmother is the only one who calls me Mikey."

"Nice to meet you," I said, making eye contact. He looked as if he was about to ask me something, and I almost said, "What?" except Hank came out just then to tell us dinner was served.

With just the four of us, Mike, Jason, Mrs. Bittner, and me, gathered around one end of the long dining room table, the empty chairs at the other end made it look as if the rest of the guests hadn't shown up for the evening. Trudy brought out the meal and then left us to serve ourselves.

After we passed around the salad, Jason asked politely about the history of the house. He could be such a suck-up when an entire college education was at stake. Mrs. Bittner's face brightened at the question, and she went on to tell us that the house was built by her grandfather for his fiancée. "It's such a romantic story," she said, clasping her hands to her heart. "His name was Herbert Walker. He designed it as a castle because he said his intended—her name was Cecilia—was going to be his queen. He worked with the architect to create the most unusual private home in the state. This house has a lot of unique features." She tapped Jason's arm. "I can show you later if you're interested."

"And even if he's *not* interested, she'll show him later." This came from Mike, speaking softly in my direction. When I looked up and met his eyes, he winked at me. I'm not usually into winks—they seem kind of sleazy to me—but it was really cute when he did it, and it made me feel like we shared a secret.

Mrs. Bittner continued. "Herbert was the one who first brought swans to the lake—it was a birthday present for Cecilia. They lived like royalty, and he doted on his wife." She sighed happily. "They donated the land for Walker Park. Have you been there?" she asked Jason, who shook his head before spearing a tomato wedge with his salad fork. "You really should see it. It's a lovely place with a big fountain in the middle and walking paths winding all around it. And they built the most incredible playground there when my boys were in their teens." She turned to me. "You've really never been to Walker Park?"

I shook my head.

"Not even to the playground, when you were younger?"

"It's not exactly close to where we live," I said. "It's way over on the rich end of town." She'd totally caught me off guard. And as usual, when that happened, I was blunt. Maybe too blunt.

Mike chuckled as if I'd made a joke, but Mrs. Bittner looked taken aback.

Jason, always one to make nice, said, "It's pretty far from where we live. My dad used to take us to Frontier Park, though."

Mrs. Bittner exhaled. "Oh yes, Frontier Park. Right off the expressway, isn't it?"

"Near it, yes," Jason said. "There's a creek that runs through it. We used to catch crayfish. And then let them go," he added, sounding as if he didn't want to offend anyone's environmental leanings.

"Crayfish," Mrs. Bittner repeated softly. She had swans, and we had crayfish. The social gap got wider the longer this evening went on.

The discussion shifted toward Mike then, thank God. Mrs. Bittner asked about his parents, who were apparently at a charitable fundraiser that night, a dinner with an auction to follow. They wouldn't be staying out too late, Mike said, because, "Tomorrow Dad leaves for a business trip to Denver. Mom's driving him to the airport."

Mrs. Bittner sighed. "Your father is so stubborn. I wish he'd let Hank drive him for this type of thing. That's what he's here for."

Mike just smiled. "Mom doesn't mind—she likes to see him off."

The main course was some kind of fish stew with French bread. It was better than I thought it would be. After that Mike and Jason carried the conversation, discussing different aspects of competitive cycling. Mike was into it, and Jason knew more about it than I realized. He and Mike tossed around technical terms and brand names that were unfamiliar to me. Mike said he ran track in high school, but he liked cycling better. "I get on that bike and I'm home," he said. "Sweet freedom."

Jason nodded like he understood. I wondered if he was comparing it to the euphoria of booting up his computer, or if he had some other interest I didn't know about. Sometimes my brother surprised me.

"Just last year I switched to a Cannondale racing bike." Mike lifted a spoonful of the stew and blew on it. "And man, is that thing fast." He glanced up and looked around the table. "Everyone should have a passion in life. You can't just sit around the house." This last comment was directed to his grandmother, but if she noticed, she didn't seem offended.

After we'd eaten, Mrs. Bittner stood up and said, "I thought it would be nice if we went into the parlor to visit." She gestured toward the doorway. "We could have a nice talk, and it would give you kids a chance to get to know each other."

Mike held up a hand. "If you don't mind, Grandma, I'd rather not. I've been sitting all day. I was thinking I might give Angie a tour of the lake on the pontoon boat." He looked at me questioningly. "If you're up to it?"

Tough to put a person on the spot. "Sure," I said, wondering where this would lead.

Mrs. Bittner frowned and said, "Wait a minute, we just ate a lovely dinner and now you're talking about kidnapping my guest and leaving?"

Michael said, "Grandma, please. You said I should come over and help entertain your company. That's what I'm doing."

"But you can't go on a boat ride now," Mrs. Bittner said. "It's raining."

"Not anymore," he said. "And it's not supposed to start up again until later."

"Even so, don't you think it would be nice if you included Angie's brother? Maybe Jason would enjoy a boat ride too."

"That's okay," Jason said. "I'd rather stay here. I don't really like boats." Oh he was a sly one, my brother. This was his opportunity to talk money, and I knew he would. He'd be working the scholarship angle before we even left the dock.

"Then I guess it's just you and me, Angie," Mike said, smiling. "This will be nice."

"Mike, why do you insist on changing things all the time? All I wanted was for us to have a nice visit here at the house."

"And we'll have a nice visit when we get back, I promise," Mike said. "I just really want to show Angie the lake. We won't be gone long at all."

Mrs. Bittner didn't look happy, but she'd apparently run out of objections. "Make sure you leave your cell phone on. And just a quick ride around the lake and come right back."

"Nothing bad will happen. It's just a boat ride." He spoke reassuringly. "We'll be back before you know it."

Chapter 12

The pontoon had comfortable padded benches and a canopy that covered two-thirds of the boat. Mike had me sit down on a bench near a bunch of life jackets and a pile of looped rope. He sat in the captain's chair, started up the engine, and steered away from the dock as easily as backing a car out of a driveway.

Over the gentle hum of the engine, I heard the sound of frogs chirping like crickets. I had a feeling Mike wanted to talk to me about something specific, but I waited for him to bring it up. I watched as he eased the boat away from shore. "You've done this before, I take it?"

Mike turned to me and grinned. "I could drive this thing with my eyes closed. But don't worry, I'll keep them open."

"Did your grandmother always have this boat?"

He shook his head. "This isn't hers—it's ours. I live over there." He pointed off in the distance. "We've only had this boat for about a year, but we've always had boats. Not yachts or anything, just smaller ones. Kayaks and sailboats and fishing boats. I can't even remember them all. When you live on a lake, that's just what you do."

I tucked my hair behind my ears to keep it from flying forward in my face.

"If you get too chilly," he said and pointed, "there's a jacket underneath there."

"I'm fine."

"My friends and I used to camp in the woods over there," he said, waving his hand toward the shore. He steered the boat slowly around the perimeter of the lake, pointing out houses and telling the stories behind them. One family had amassed their fortune producing sausage. Others were in printing, banking, or real estate. Another mansion dweller owned the largest brewery in the state at one time.

"Have you lived on the lake your whole life?" I asked.

"Almost. My dad bought our house when I was little so we could keep an eye on my grandmother and Uncle Scott." He glanced over at me. "Just so you know, my parents and I feel terrible about what happened to you. Scott was gone for a long time, and he seemed better when he came back. We really had no idea he was capable of violence."

I nodded and turned my head toward the far side of the lake. Music floated across the lake and then faded, as if someone had opened and shut a door. I looked in the direction it came from and saw a stream of lights, like Christmas lights hanging above a row of boats in a slip. "Someone's having a party," I said.

"Nope, that's the neighborhood eyesore," Mike said, grinning. "Zap's Bar and Restaurant. It started out being a place for fishermen to get a beer and a burger, but now it's a biker hangout. Over the years people on the lake have tried to get it closed down, but they never succeeded."

He shifted into a lower gear, so now we were at trolling speed. I looked out over the ripples and waves and wondered about the whole world of life in the water below. If I could have reached, I would have trailed my fingertips in the water. Mike too was quiet. For several minutes we both looked out over the water. The gentle movement of the boat was calming.

Mike cleared his throat. "I had a reason for asking you out on the boat." He moved the lever so the boat was only idling and turned to face me. "I wanted to talk to you without my grandmother around."

"Really? What about?"

"There are some things you should know about my uncle, off the record."

"I'm all ears."

Michael leaned forward with elbows on knees and looked at me over steepled fingers. "It's kind of involved, and I think I'd rather tell you somewhere inside. How would you feel about going to Zap's? We could get something to drink, and I can give you the whole story."

He definitely had my attention. "Okay," I said.

"And we can talk about how she got you to come out to the house. I can only imagine what she pulled to make that happen." He straightened up and turned back to the wheel before I could ask what he meant.

Chapter 13

Zap's Bar and Restaurant was as fancy as it sounds. A bar off to one side was filled with young guys drinking beer and watching some sports thing on TV. The rest of the room was filled with a row of booths and a few tables. The music I'd heard earlier came from a jukebox, a 1950s throwback. A young couple intertwined in lust sat at the only occupied table. She sat on his lap with her arms draped around his neck. His head rested on her chest. Mike and I took a booth and ordered Cokes and onion rings from a waitress who didn't look thrilled when we said that was all we were having.

I was just thinking how surreal this whole scenario was when Mike said, "This is kind of weird, don't you think? Us being here together because of what my uncle did. And then him killing himself. Bizarre."

"Yes, it's bizarre all right," I said. "But you know what? I know this sounds terrible, but I can't help it—I'm kind of glad your uncle is dead."

The words came out, and I immediately regretted saying them because it made me sound like an awful person. But Mike wasn't shocked. "I don't blame you," he said. "If I put myself in your shoes, I'd probably feel the same way."

"Thanks for understanding," I said. "I can't help feeling that way. I'm not really a bad person. I've just been through a lot."

Mike said, "I didn't think you were a bad person. Anyone who'd been stalked and beaten half to death like you were would feel the same way."

Stalked? I looked at him, puzzled. "What?"

The waitress came back with our Cokes. "Your onion rings will be here soon," she said, setting down the drinks and our straws, still in their paper wrappers.

"Mike? Why did you say he stalked me?"

"I'm going to tell you something," he said slowly, "because I think you deserve to know. You have to promise, though, that you won't tell anyone you heard it from me. If it gets back to me, I'll deny telling you, okay?"

"Okay, I guess."

"My parents would kill me. It's a family secret. I think they're afraid of lawsuits. They think the less said, the better."

"Mike, you're starting to freak me out. Just tell me."

He leaned forward, palms flat on the table. "This all happened years ago. I heard about it from my mom. My Uncle Scott was fixated on your mother, for some reason. Right after your mom disappeared, he started keeping a scrapbook of all the newspaper articles about it. He wrote some short stories and made her the main character. He also went through the library's collection of high school yearbooks and cut out all the photos of your mom."

I felt the blood drain from my face. "No way." I thought about Mrs. Bittner's comment about how much I looked like my mother. Now it made sense.

"Yeah, it's true." Mike took the wrapper off his straw and stuck it into his glass. "My grandmother made a sizeable donation to the library to hush it up."

"But how did he know my mother?"

"My dad said he *didn't* know her. He just saw her around town and became obsessed with her. He admitted to all this stuff later on—how he made phone calls to her pretending to be a telemarketer, and how he used to drive past your place at night, hoping he'd see her through the window."

"Wait a minute—the obsession started before she disappeared?"

"Yeah, we think so. It's hard to say because Uncle Scott didn't always make sense."

My heart pounded. All these years I'd been sure my mother was still alive. Even when other people told me the chances were slim, I still believed she was out there. My last thought every night was a prayer that she would come home to us, safe and sound. So many times after making my request, I'd heard her voice in my mind, praying for the same thing. I'd been positive she was out there, but now hearing what Mike had to say about his uncle, my belief was shaken. "Mike, did he kill my mom?"

"I don't really know, Angie." He looked sad. "A few weeks after your mom disappeared, Uncle Scott got sent away for a long time to a treatment center. Then he was in some group home and only came back to visit once in a while. I'm not sure of the details. He'd only been back living on the lake for a month or two before he attacked you. He always said he had nothing to do with your mom's disappearance, and my grandmother believed him."

"So the police never questioned him?"

"Nope, nobody outside of the family even knew. My parents only found out in bits and pieces, and I didn't even know any of it until recently. My mom told me after Uncle Scott was arrested."

"Really." I had a hundred questions, but for the moment I was speechless.

"I actually don't know my grandmother too well. My dad checks in on her from time to time, but otherwise we kind of avoid her. It's weird over at her house—like the Addams Family or something. My mom doesn't like me spending too much time there, and she hates that Hank, but since Dad's business hasn't been doing so well and Grandma is paying for my college tuition next year, I've been going over more lately."

"Why does your mom hate Hank?"

"You haven't noticed he's kind of creepy?" Mike asked. "My mom thinks there's some weird dynamic between Hank and Trudy and my grandmother. When I come over, Hank sort of acts..." Here he paused. "Like he belongs there more than I do. Like he resents me being there."

I'd noticed it too—the way Hank hovered possessively around Mrs. Bittner, more like a concerned husband than an employee.

Mike continued. "And then there's the fact that my grandmother hasn't left the house in ages. That's why I knew she wouldn't come out on the pontoon. She hasn't stepped outside in years. It's like the house has some hold on her or something."

I was trying hard to process all of this. My mind was still whirring with the news that Scott Bittner was obsessed with my mother. "So Scott picked me because I'm her daughter and I look like her?"

"I think so." He took a sip of his soda. "And Grandma feels guilty about it, so she'll try to make it up to you somehow. Watch out or she'll be worming her way into your life."

He didn't have to worry about me. As soon as we got back, I was having Hank drive us home. And when my grandmother returned from her cruise, we were contacting the police and telling them what I'd heard. Even though Scott was dead, they could still follow up and see what they could find out about his connection to my mother. Maybe, after all this time, we could get some answers.

The waitress slid the plate of onion rings onto our table as she went by, but they didn't tempt me. In fact, the thought of eating made me nauseous. Mike offered me one, and I shook my head.

"Are you sorry I told you?" he asked, sounding worried.

"No," I said. I couldn't say much more because my heart started racing like a cranked engine. At the same time, I was overcome with dizziness. I looked beyond Mike, trying to fix my eyes on something still, but all I could see was that damn couple in a lip-lock.

I knew I was having another panic attack, but knowing it didn't make it stop. I tried breathing like the nurse showed me in the hospital, without looking too obvious.

"What are you doing?" Mike asked.

I shook my head, like *I can't talk to you now.* In and out, in and out—I kept my air intake steady. If I concentrated enough on my breathing, maybe I wouldn't die in a seedy restaurant across from the nephew of the man who ruined my life and maybe killed my mother.

"Are you having trouble breathing?"

I moved my head up and down like one of those drinking bird toys and kept my breathing steady, as if my life depended on it.

"Do you have asthma?"

I shook my head.

"Allergies?"

I had the feeling I could keel over dead waiting for him to guess correctly. Exasperated, I choked out the words, "Anxiety attack."

His face took on a serious look I hadn't seen before. "You're sure it's an anxiety attack? You've had this before?"

"In the hospital."

"Did they prescribe anything for it?"

"No."

He looked around the room. "Would it help to go outside?"

I gripped the edges of the table. It was the only thing holding me together. "No."

"My mom gets these. I know what to do. Here, hold on to me." He said it so authoritatively I didn't even consider not doing it. Reaching across the table, Mike encased my hands in his, warm fingers pressing against my palms. I was sweating now as if I'd hiked up a steep incline. "You're going to be fine," he said. "This will only last a few more minutes." Even over the sound of the music, his voice was strong. "Look right at my eyes, and keep breathing slow and steady. You're going to be fine."

I followed his directions, even though I felt like dropping to the floor and curling up into a fetal position. I noticed for the first time that his eyes were blue, a muted sky blue like you see in watercolor paintings.

"You're doing great. Just keep it up."

I gasped a little. He pressed my hands gently and said, "Stop thinking. Just breathe and keep your eyes on me. Just a few more minutes. You'll gradually feel better and better, and then you'll be fine."

I did keep my eyes on his face, not an easy task with the guys at the bar arguing over some bit of sports trivia and the young lovers behind Mike getting disentangled and pushing their one shared chair up against the table. I'd somehow linked them with my attack. I was glad they were leaving.

"It's almost over," Mike said. "You're going to feel your heart rate slowing down. You'll find it easier to breathe. Keep going, you're getting there."

I concentrated on my breathing. *In out, in out, in out.* Odd that so much of life depended on this one normally unconscious action. Now it was like I'd switched from automatic to manual.

"Doing fine," he said, in the same way nurses reassure children getting shots.

We sat there like that for at least two songs on the jukebox, him holding my hands like he was just about to propose marriage, and me concentrating on my breathing.

"You're feeling better, aren't you?" he asked finally.

I forced my head up and down, but I didn't trust myself to say the words aloud. I felt fine now, but everything could change in an instant, it seemed.

He looked around the room, breaking the link between our eyes. "It's kind of stuffy in here. What do you say we go? You might feel better when we get outside." He released my hands, and my fingers uncurled reflexively. I got up from the table while Mike pulled a twenty out of his wallet. He left the bill on the table, and we headed out.

"Night, folks," the bartender called as the screen door slammed behind us.

The temperature had dropped since our arrival. The night air was humid but cool. I shivered as I got myself onto the bench seat of the boat. Mike dug around in a compartment underneath and located a lightweight jacket, which he draped across my shoulders. "I was trying to help by telling you about my uncle," he said. "If it were me, I'd want to know. I didn't mean to freak you out."

I pulled the jacket closer. "It's okay. I'm glad you told me."

"Just watch it with my grandmother. She's really a sad case. Talk about needy. She'll pull you right into her web if you let her."

I nodded.

"I'd better get you back," he said. "Grandma must be having a meltdown by now."

Chapter 14

I'd never had problems with boats, never been seasick or had motion sickness or whatever you want to call it. This time, though, was different. My anxiety attack had left me feeling weak and disoriented. The lake was relatively calm, but my stomach lurched with every dip and rise. I was dizzy too, but at least my heart had stopped pounding and I could breathe. I thought about Dad's story, the one where he was trapped in the elevator and got so panicked he had to drop down and put his head between his knees. At least I didn't do that at Zap's. Thank God for small favors.

I clutched the side of the boat and waited for the dizziness to subside. Mike tried to make small talk, but I wasn't much in the mood, and it was hard to converse while he was driving, so I just listened. He'd heard Dad's band play somewhere and thought they were really good. It was true. They were really good, but lots of bands are just as good and never go anywhere. It was all a crapshoot, according to Dad. I closed my eyes and let the breeze flow over my face. I'd feel better after a good night's sleep.

By the time we reached the Bittner dock, I felt even worse. Mike tied up the moor lines while I climbed out of the boat. Something was definitely wrong. My muscles weren't cooperating, and my head felt like it would explode from the pressure.

Getting out of the boat, I lost my footing on the wet boards and fell down, like an idiot. Even worse, I felt my ankle buckle and snap in pain as I hit the deck. "Owww!" I cried out in pain. Tears filled my eyes.

Mike was at my side in a moment, but it was too late. "Whoa, Angie, are you okay?" He sounded frightened.

"Oh my God," I said, "I think I broke something." It was hard to tell what I could have broken. My whole foot hurt like hell.

Mike helped me up, but I couldn't put any weight on my right side. I looped an arm around his shoulder. "I can't believe I fell. I feel so stupid." We trudged slowly to the house. Halfway there, Hank came out of the darkness to meet us.

"She hurt her ankle," Mike said. Hank wordlessly went to my other side, and they both helped me the rest of the way.

Mrs. Bittner met us at the door. "What happened?" Her shrill voice made the pain worse.

"It's nothing," I said through gritted teeth, but at the same time Mike was telling them how I fell and Mrs. Bittner was squawking that we never should have gone on the boat.

"Hank, take her into the parlor," she said. And then to Mike she said, "I told you not to be out too long. I knew it was a bad idea. And I've been trying to call you, but you didn't have your phone on."

"I'm sorry. I didn't realize it was off."

Hank lowered me onto the sofa, and I saw my brother's face right above me. "Angie, are you okay?"

"I'm okay," I said, ignoring the white-hot searing pain coming from my foot. "I think I just need some ibuprofen."

Despite my attempts to downplay the situation, things went out of control after that. Jason and Mike and I argued for getting me home to bed, but Mrs. Bittner would have none of it.

"She needs to see a doctor," she said and then snapped her fingers at Hank. "Get Brimley on the phone and tell him we need him out here *immediately*. It's an emergency." And then she patted my hair. "Don't you worry about a thing, Angel. Grandma is taking care of everything." I caught the word "Grandma," and even through the pain and my mental anguish it struck me as odd and familiar. As if she had made herself an honorary family member. Mike caught the reference too, and he scrunched up his forehead, puzzled. I think he was about to say something to her, but she was busy insisting I recline, adjusting the throw pillow and all the while making *tsk-tsk* noises.

By the time the doctor arrived, I felt a little better—sitting up and reassuring everyone who would listen that I was just fine, it was nothing, really. Even though Dr. Brimley was a nice old guy who could have been Santa's twin, I hated that this had turned into a major production. The doctor examined my foot, which looked a little puffy by then, and asked me to flex my toes, which I did. He listened to my heart and lungs, took my pulse, and checked my blood pressure. He finally concluded that it wasn't broken, just sprained. "Doesn't look too serious," he said. "Elevate it as much as possible for the next day or two. Crutches or a cane would help if you do have to move around. Ice it periodically. You can wrap it with an Ace bandage if that alleviates the pain. If the swelling doesn't go down by tomorrow, give me a call."

Mrs. Bittner hovered over me as he examined me and fussed over the doctor as he prepared to leave. "I can't thank you enough for coming out, Doctor."

"No problem at all, Lillian," he said, snapping shut his bag. "It's the least I can do after all your family has done for the hospital."

"You know, I've been meaning to call you," she said, leaning toward him, "because I've been having some trouble sleeping lately."

"Would you like me to call in a refill for your pills?" Dr. Brimley asked.

Mrs. Bittner nodded. "That would be very nice."

After the doctor left, I assumed we could go home, but I assumed wrong. Mrs. Bittner insisted she talk to Dad, and then Jason let it slip that he was in California, and all hell broke loose. "No one is home with you kids?" she asked, horrified.

I had a very bad feeling about this. I gave Jason the stink-eye, but he was too busy doing damage control to notice. "It's only until Sunday," Jason said. "And he calls us every day."

"Oh, I don't like this at all." Her voice was very disapproving. I had a fleeting thought that she might call social services and get Dad in trouble. Oh, if that happened, we were completely screwed.

"Grandma, it's okay." Mike put an arm around her shoulder. "My parents leave me alone overnight all the time, and it always works out just fine. Jason and Angie seem very responsible." I flashed him a smile of appreciation.

"That's all well and good, Mikey," she said, "but Angie is injured, and it happened at my house. I can't let her leave here unsupervised. I wouldn't feel right about it. Angie and Jason are staying here tonight, and that's final." Her voice was firm.

"Do you think that's such a good idea, ma'am?" Hank stepped forward.

"I said they're staying. End of discussion." Her tone left no room for compromise. "Hank, you can take Jason back to their apartment to get a few things. Mr. Favorite can pick them up here when he gets back from his trip on Sunday."

Sunday? That would mean we'd be staying two nights. "Wait a minute," I said. "I think we need to call my dad. He's expecting us to be home." Mrs. Bittner sighed and folded her arm, but didn't object. I nodded toward my brother, who pulled out his phone and made the call. When I saw his face fall, I knew he didn't get through. "I got voice mail," he said finally. We all listened as he left a brief message explaining what had happened. Even though Jason said to call back right away, I wasn't hopeful. Dad sometimes forgot to turn his phone on when he wasn't using it. He wasn't really the type to keep up with things.

"Well, then that's it," Mrs. Bittner said. "You'll stay the night."

I looked at Jason, mentally pleading for him to get us out of this.

"But I have to work tomorrow," Jason said. "My boss is going to pick me up at seven thirty." He said it like that would get us off the hook.

"Hank will drive you home at seven tomorrow morning." Mrs. Bittner turned to Hank. "I don't feel comfortable letting these two children stay by themselves. Especially with Angie having a sprained ankle and it being our fault."

Neither Jason nor I were okay with this, but without a car of our own, we weren't going anywhere. Mike glanced at his grandmother and then shrugged in my direction, like, *See, what did I tell you?* Clearly he wasn't going to help. In only a few hours' time, Mrs. Bittner had managed to worm her way into our lives, just like he predicted.

After Jason and Hank left, Mrs. Bittner cleared her throat and said, "Thank you for coming to dinner, Mikey. We won't be keeping you any longer."

I had the feeling he was in trouble because of me and our boat trip. He took his cue and said goodnight to his grandmother, then came over to me and slipped a scrap of paper with his cell number on it into my palm. "I'm right across the lake," he whispered, his eyes meeting mine. "Call if you need something."

Chapter 15

Jason and I would sleep in separate bedrooms on the second floor, joined in the middle by a common bathroom, Mrs. Bittner explained. She helped me up to my room on the second floor and gave me a nightgown, one of hers. It was lovely, and I was really excited about wearing it. Not. She also left me with an ice pack and a pair of ancient crutches left over from when her son Michael had broken a leg when he was in eighth grade. She waited while I tried them out, and when I'd taken a few steps she exclaimed, "Just the right size for your height! We couldn't have planned it any better."

Lucky me. "They'll do," I said.

"Now, I'll be right down the hall if you need anything, so don't hesitate to come and get me. I'll leave my door open a crack—just come right in," Mrs. Bittner said, smiling.

"Okay, thanks," I said, wondering how it came to this. *What I did on my summer vacation, by Angie Favorite.* A true nightmare.

"Goodnight then, Angie. Sleep tight, don't let the bedbugs bite." She sounded positively giddy. For a second, I thought she was going to try to hug or kiss me, but I turned away before that could happen. After she shut the door, I could tell from her footsteps that she waited outside for a while before walking away.

I hobbled over to the bed and sank down in despair. How did this happen? Oh, I was so angry with myself for getting sick and falling, and I was pissed off with Jason for talking me into coming here in the first place. He'd made it all sound so simple. *What do we have to lose? Hank picks us up, we eat a good meal, you talk nice to the grandson, and maybe, just maybe, we both end up with full-ride scholarships.* Easy in theory, but I should have known better. If only I'd listened to my instincts instead of letting him guilt me into doing something I didn't want to do. And for all I knew, he never did find out about college scholarships.

Tomorrow I was going to call my friend Maria and see if her parents would pick us up. If not them, then Uncle Bob for sure. I wasn't staying here for more than one night. Even one night was too much. I was sure I wouldn't be able to sleep at all in this creepy place. The air had that dusty smell, the kind that sticks in your nose when you open up old boxes in an attic. I wanted to take a shower, but there was no way I was getting naked in the Bittner house. I wanted to go home more than anything else in the world.

An hour later I was under the covers, listening to the rain pound against the window, when I heard footsteps in the hall outside my door. I held my breath when the door opened. "Angie?" It was Jason, whispering. Finally he was back from our apartment.

I sat up. "Yes?"

"I brought you something." He opened the door a little wider, letting in some light from the hallway. I saw something drop from his arms, and then the thing shot across the floor and up onto the bed. My kitty.

"Oh Misty." I scratched behind her ears, and she rubbed against my arm like she wanted to crawl inside me. "Just what

I needed. Thanks! I can't believe you brought her." Her purring was my favorite sound.

Jason flipped on the light switch and closed the door behind him. "Yeah, Hank thought it was kind of weird, but I didn't want to leave her alone at the apartment. I figured you'd like it if she was here." He came in and sat on the edge of the bed. "Angie, I'm really sorry I talked you into coming here for dinner, but the good news is that we're a sure thing for the scholarships."

I narrowed my eyes at him and stuck out my tongue. "Thanks, Einstein. If we ever get out of here alive, I'm sure I'll appreciate it."

Jason said, "Please don't be mad, Angie. I mean, God, I had no idea we'd wind up staying overnight. I know I should have figured out a way to get us out of here, but it all happened so fast. Tomorrow I'm going to call Dad again and see what we should do. I'm sure Uncle Bob would come and pick us up. Hank said if we had a ride he'd help us get out of the house, but he'd have to do it behind Mrs. Bittner's back." He reached over and rubbed behind Misty's ears. "He doesn't want to lose his job."

"You wouldn't believe what Mike Bittner told me about his Uncle Scott," I said. Then I told him the whole thing, how Scott had been obsessed with our mother and how Mrs. Bittner had spirited her son away after our mother's disappearance. Jason didn't say anything, but I watched the expression on his face change from fascination to horror.

"Oh my God," he said. "Do you think Scott killed her?"

"I don't know, but I think we should call the police as soon as we get out of here," I said. "I really didn't want to come here to begin with, and now that I know about Scott's obsession with Mom it's even worse."

"I know." He sighed. "But I don't know any way around it. It's so late, and we're here now. If you could walk and the weather was better, we could just leave and call a friend to pick us up, but the way it is now..."

"We're stuck," I said glumly.

"Yeah, I'm sorry. But it's just for tonight," he said and then gave me an odd look. "Are you sleeping in your clothes?"

"Yeah. Mrs. Bittner gave me one of her nightgowns, but there's no way."

"I brought a bag of your stuff." Jason left my side and went out into the hallway. He returned with a plastic bag and Misty's carrier and litter box, and then he carefully closed the door and locked it. "Your makeup case and that face cleanser stuff from the shower, and some clothes. Even your pajamas."

"And my toothbrush?"

"Oops." He fake-chuckled. "Sorry." Seeing the look on my face, he said, "But you know what you could do? Take the toothpaste and use your finger to kind of squish it around. I've done that. It works, kind of."

"You remembered the toothpaste, but not the toothbrushes?" And he was supposed to be the genius in the family.

"I only forgot *your* toothbrush."

"Oh great. You remembered your own but not mine? Honestly, Jason, where's your brain?"

"I'm sorry, Angie. I was just sort of rattled. Hank was standing there waiting, and I was trying to think of what to bring. Then I had to grab Misty's stuff, and then I tried to call Dad again, but I still got his voice mail. There was a lot to remember." Jason smiled. "But aren't you glad I brought your buddy here?" He reached over and rubbed her belly. "She was so sad without you."

"Yeah, I'm glad she's here."

"I figured I'd set up her litter box and food in the bathroom, and we'd keep the doors to the hallway shut and locked, okay?"

"Okay."

"If you need anything during the night, just holler. I'll leave the doors to the bathroom open so I can hear you."

Having Jason close by was one consolation. At least I wasn't alone. "Do you think you could skip work tomorrow, or go in later, after we've figured out who can come and get us?"

Jason shook his head. "I already took off so much time when you were in the hospital, and I really don't want to do it again. But I promise I'll make some calls first thing. We'll be out of here in no time at all."

Chapter 16

Jason's idea of no time at all seemed like infinity. He said
good-bye before he left. I meant to get up then, but I fell
back asleep and was completely out of it until midmorning.
I washed up in the bathroom and changed into some clean
clothes. I debated whether or not to use the crutches, and then I
decided against it. My foot felt better, and if I kept most of my
weight off it, I was okay.

I was in a feisty mood. Today was the day I'd ask
Mrs. Bittner about Scott's obsession with my mother. Part of me
didn't want to piss her off and mess up our chances to get a possible scholarship, but given the choice, I'd rather know the truth
about my mother than get my college tuition paid for. Each of
us had some money saved, which was a start. Jason could probably get a scholarship somewhere based on his SAT and ACT
scores alone. And our family's low-income bracket had to make
us eligible for some kind of grant or loan.

The elevator still shimmied and made that strange straining noise, but I guess I was getting used to it because it didn't
freak me out quite as much this time. When I went down the
hallway toward the kitchen, I heard voices—a man and woman
talking. The conversation sounded tense. I went as slowly as I
could, which was pretty easy considering my foot still hurt like
hell. I was thankful for the thick hallway runner that muffled

my steps. I stopped when I got close enough to catch what they were saying.

"I just don't like this—I don't like it at all," Hank was saying. I held my breath and flattened myself against the wall to listen. "If this whole thing comes out, no one in the world would believe we weren't involved. And mark my words, we're the ones who'll end up in jail, and she'll walk, free as a bird. That's the way it works. I'm tempted to call it quits while we still can. Get in the car and just get the hell out of here."

"And go where?" This came from Trudy.

"Far, far away."

"After all these years and all we've done?" Trudy said. "Hank, get a hold of yourself." Unlike her husband, she didn't sound worried at all. "We worked for how many years to keep this a secret? And we end up with nothing? I don't think so."

Hank paced around the room—I heard his footsteps against the wood floor. "I have no idea how you can be so calm."

Their voices were getting quieter. I had to strain to hear. Trudy said, "She promised the big payout at the end of the year. We get the money then and we're gone. Hang in there for just a little while longer." What were they talking about?

"I just have a bad feeling," Hank said glumly.

"Oh my word, you're fussing about nothing. Remember, we're in control. The kids' father will pick them up on Sunday, and everything will be back to normal." Trudy was stirring something. I heard a spoon clinking against a metal bowl.

"We might not even have to wait that long," Hank said. "The boy is going to try to get someone to pick them up today. I told him I'd try to talk Lillian into it, and if that doesn't work I'd do my best to sneak them out of the house."

Trudy harrumphed. "Good luck with that. You can't get that she-devil to do anything she doesn't want to do, and it doesn't take much to set her off, either. One of these days she's going to do some serious damage with that gun she likes to wave around."

Hank said, "Lillian wouldn't shoot anyone. I know how to handle her, don't worry. I think I can even convince her that it's too risky to keep the kids here another night, that she should really let them go back to their apartment."

"Yeah, like that's going to work," Trudy said. "Why don't you just drive them home yourself if you're so worried?"

"There's no way I'd take a chance like that," Hank said. "She checks the odometer. She's crazy, but she's not stupid. She'd figure it out."

I heard noises like the movement of dishware and the opening and closing of a refrigerator door. The couple started talking about their schedule for the day. Hank said the landscapers were coming soon and needed to be supervised. Especially, he said, "After how they screwed up last time."

He told his wife to keep an eye on me, and she laughed dismissively and said, "Not happening. I'm doing enough baby-sitting as it is—I'm not doing any more." When Trudy started up the dishwasher and I heard the sound of a door opening and shutting, I eased my way back down the hallway. When I got twenty feet away, I did a U-turn and headed back to the kitchen, this time walking normally and humming softly so they could hear me coming. When I walked in, I saw Trudy hugging a large, stainless-steel bowl to her midsection, stirring the contents with her free hand. She was a tiny woman, shorter than me even, and today her shoulder-length brown hair was held back in a hair net. She glanced up when I came through the doorway. "Morning, Angie."

"Good morning, Trudy. Where is everyone?"

Trudy said she wasn't sure where Mrs. Bittner was, but that Hank was outside getting ready for the landscaping crew. She pointed to the back door, which explained the noise of Hank's exit and why I hadn't passed him in the hall. "Would you like some breakfast?" she asked and offered to make me eggs and bacon. I politely took a pass and had a bowl of cereal instead.

As I watched her making homemade granola, I thought how odd it was that she'd just been discussing a crime that could put her and Hank in jail. It was a big secret about something that had been going on for years, but that's all I got out of the conversation. I desperately wanted to know more but wasn't sure how I could find out. Still, I wanted to work my way toward finding out whatever I could, especially if it involved Scott Bittner and my mother. I decided to ease into it with some polite conversation. "Do you like working here?" I asked Trudy.

"Of course I do." She was concentrating now on spreading chunks of granola onto a baking pan. I watched as a stray walnut chunk bounced onto the table.

"But you don't mind being in someone else's house all the time? I would think it would be kind of awkward."

"What's awkward about it?" Trudy broke up a large chunk with a spatula.

"I mean, what if Mrs. Bittner decided she didn't want you working here anymore? Then you'd be out of a job *and* out of a place to live."

"She'd never do that."

"But how can you be sure? It happens all the time. People get fired, they get laid off, they get in fights with their boss."

"Nothing like that would happen here," Trudy said, palms flat on the table. "Mrs. Bittner counts on us to keep everything running smoothly. She'd be lost without us."

I dipped my spoon into my cereal bowl and slowly stirred my Cheerios. "After thirty years here, I bet you know everything there is to know about the Bittners."

Trudy shrugged and returned to her work. "I don't know about that. We do our work and mind our own business. If it doesn't concern us, we don't go prying." She gave me a hard look. "That's good advice for anyone."

I pressed on. "But you knew about Scott, right?"

"What about Scott?"

"Did you know Scott was obsessed with my mother, Laura Favorite? Do you know anything about that?"

She put a hand to her forehead and looked down at the table. "Oh no, don't be starting up with that. I don't need any aggravation from you. I told you I just mind my own business." Her eyes closed. "Look what you did now. I have a sudden pain in my head, right behind my left eye. That's just how my migraines start. Oh, I hope you haven't triggered one. That would be inexcusable."

"Trudy," I said more firmly, "do you know what happened to my mother? Did Scott murder her?"

Trudy looked pale. She exhaled loudly and answered without meeting my eyes. "Scott had a lot of problems, but he wouldn't kill anybody. He was a very sweet boy."

Oh man, I was tired of hearing good things about Scott Bittner. "He wasn't so sweet to me," I said. My voice was getting louder, I knew, but I couldn't help myself. "You know he attacked me, right? He grabbed me in a parking lot and dragged me up a hill. He gave me a skull fracture." Technically not true since the skull fracture was a result of my fall down the hill, but still, that only happened because of Scott. "He would have killed me if there hadn't been witnesses."

"He wouldn't have killed you." Now her voice matched mine. "Don't be ridiculous. He never would have done such a thing. You don't know the half of it."

"What's the half of it?"

Trudy's lips clamped together, and I knew the conversation was over. "I need to go take my medication. Help yourself to whatever you need."

After she left the room, I put my bowl and spoon in the sink. Through the window I saw Hank out back talking to two men in green shirts. He glanced in my direction and frowned at the sight of me in the window. If only my psychic powers had kicked in just then. I would have loved to know what was on his mind.

Chapter 17

It was time to have a heart-to-heart talk with Mrs. Bittner. If I wasn't going to stay at the castle much longer, I needed answers now. I searched the house, walking slowly through the ground floor, no small feat with my still swollen ankle. When I didn't find her, I decided to try upstairs. I took the elevator up and checked on Misty first then went down the hall to Mrs. Bittner's room. I found her door shut, making me sure she was inside.

I knocked on the door, tentatively at first, and then a bit louder. I leaned against the doorframe and kept rapping until my knuckles stung. The door vibrated in its frame, but there was no answer.

I was still knocking when Hank came up behind me, so silently he scared the crap out of me.

"If you're looking for Mrs. Bittner, you're in the wrong place," he said, his voice in my ear. "She's not in her room."

"She's not?" Sheepishly I dropped my arm down to my side. "Where is she? I need to talk to her."

Hank gave me a haughty look. "Mrs. Bittner has some other business to attend to. She's going to be rather busy for the next several hours and doesn't want to be disturbed."

"I'll talk to her at lunch, then," I said.

"I'm taking her meal up on a tray," he said. "And aren't you supposed to stay off your feet and keep that ankle elevated? If you'd like to read in the library, I'd be glad to bring you a glass of lemonade."

We were eye to eye now. Leaning with my back against the door, I felt trapped. "Lemonade would be nice," I said finally and found myself reluctantly following him to the library.

There was a time when spending a few hours in a library with a glass of lemonade would have worked for me. Funny how life changes. I wasn't so thrilled with library-time now, but at least I could sit and make a phone call. Jason had to have talked to someone by now. If not, I could make a few calls of my own.

It was a good idea, but the battery was low in my phone, and I didn't have the charger. I was able to text Jason, who probably wouldn't get it until his lunch break, but after that my phone died. I could have asked to use Mrs. Bittner's house phone, but I was growing mistrustful of everything in the castle. Someone might be listening in. No, I'd wait to hear from my brother first.

I settled back in the comfy library chair and took a sip of the lemonade Hank had brought after he'd made sure I was parked where he wanted me. The glass was frosted, and the drink was kind of tart and had a lot of pulp—not my favorite, frankly, but it was still pretty good. I flipped through a few books in the library. Nothing interested me, and I was too wired to sit in one spot for very long.

What was I doing here? Stuck in the library because that's what Hank wanted? Mike was right, he was kind of creepy, especially now that I'd heard what he and his wife were talking about in the kitchen. They would go to jail for sure if they were found out, they'd said. I had a sick feeling about all this.

I was lost in thought when I heard footsteps approach. I lifted my head and peered around the back of my chair, expecting to see Mrs. Bittner, then I did a double take when Mike came into the room.

"Hey, Angie." His voice was upbeat. He sat down in the chair opposite me. "How're you doing?" Oh man, he was even cuter than I remembered.

"I thought you might be your grandmother," I said.

"Ah, that would explain the look on your face when I first walked in."

"What kind of look did I have on my face?"

He laughed. "You looked kind of weirded-out, actually."

"I am weirded-out." I wanted to tell him what I'd over-heard Trudy and Hank talking about, but something stopped me. Better to wait until I was out of the house. The whole thing could blow up if Mike told his grandmother.

"So I take it you're not a happy houseguest?"

"I'm not too thrilled to be here, if you must know. And I par-tially blame you." I shifted in my chair. "When all this happened last night you said nothing. You could have helped, you know."

"I did say I thought you and your brother would be fine at home," Mike said. "I tried to convince her, really I did."

"Yeah, for like a second. And then you left. You could have driven us home if you'd wanted to." I wasn't letting him off the hook, even if he was really cute.

"In what? My pontoon boat?" His face grew serious. "Angie, I don't have a car. I got two speeding tickets a couple of weeks ago, and my dad grounded me off the car. Honestly, if I could have, I would have offered to take you home. But I knew once my grandmother got that tone in her voice she wasn't budging for anything."

I tapped on the padded arm of the chair and watched as dust motes rose upwards. "So basically you're no help at all."

Mike smiled. "You're being pretty grouchy considering I'm just about to help you out here."

"How's that?"

"I brought my mom. She's going to talk to Grandma, and then we're going to take you back to your place."

I sat up straight. "Really?"

"Really, really," Mike said, looking pretty pleased with himself.

"Oh my God, you're my hero." He was getting better looking with every passing minute.

"That's me, the hero. We would have come last night, but my folks were out until midnight, so we put it off until this morning. My dad had to leave for his business trip, so Mom and I came right after we dropped him off at the airport."

I got up. "I have to pack and get Jason's stuff together too. My cat is here. Can you help me get her into her carrier? It's easier with two people, and—"

"Whoa, wait a minute." He got up and put his hand on the small of my back. "Not just yet. I have my instructions. We're supposed to sit tight until we hear it's a go. My grandmother can be pretty testy, so we're better off just letting my mom handle her. Don't poke the monkey if you don't have to, as my dad says."

"Okay." I sank back into my chair. "How long do you think it will take?"

He shrugged. "Your guess is as good as mine."

A half an hour later we still hadn't heard from Mike's mom, but I didn't mind being holed up in the library anymore. Just knowing we were leaving soon improved my mood. Mike went to the kitchen and got two new glasses of lemonade, and we both settled in for the wait. We talked about bands that were going to be playing at The Rave in Milwaukee, and it turned out we had similar tastes. Milwaukee was two hours away, but I'd gone there with friends a few times when there was a group I wanted to see. Mike was getting tickets to see a band I liked, and I found myself sort of agreeing to go with him and his friends in August. "Your girlfriend won't mind if I go with you?" I asked. Oh, I was sly.

Mike shook his head. "I don't have a girlfriend. I am all alone in life." He pulled the corners of his mouth down—a clown frown. It made me laugh. As we grinned at each other, I felt that click you get when you hit it off with someone you don't know very well but would like to know better.

Who could have predicted this? I couldn't wait to tell my friends I was going out with a group of almost-college guys and maybe one in particular. And that particular guy happened to be related to the man who'd attacked me. Even now I had trouble believing it. Just yesterday I'd known him only as Scott Bittner's nephew, and now I was able to separate him for who he was—Mike, just Mike. Life takes funny turns sometimes.

He told me about his summer job as a towel attendant at the club. For a rich boy, he had kind of a scut job. His parents believed in having him learn the value of a dollar, he said. Recently he'd graduated from towel duty to cleaning the locker rooms, so we had another thing in common. I told him about my work cleaning offices and the things I found in wastebaskets. "You wouldn't believe it," I said. "I've seen used condoms, personal notes, photos. One time a framed baby photo was in the garbage. I thought it must have fallen in there by mistake, so I took it out. The next time I cleaned it was in there again, so I guess they really meant to get rid of it."

"Weird," he said. "Was it an ugly baby?"

"No, it wasn't ugly. Babies aren't ugly. Some are just cuter than others."

"I bet you were a really cute baby," he said. Oh my God, I couldn't believe he was flirting with me when I totally looked like crap.

"Yeah, I was. People came from all around to see me because I was *so* cute." I tucked my hair behind my ear and gave him a smile.

"You still are really cute."

I felt my face getting red, which I hated. I never blushed, and I mean never. The only time I could remember doing it was in seventh grade when this girl handed me an *Elle* magazine in the cafeteria and told me to look at page twenty-seven. "You won't believe it," she'd said. Stupidly, I flipped to page twenty-seven, where someone had pasted a large photo of a naked guy. I turned beet red and dropped the magazine, and that was all anyone at school talked about for days. That was the one and only time I ever remembered blushing, until now. I swallowed and tried to deflect attention away from my reddening face. "So were you a cute baby?"

"Oh yeah. People came from all over to see me too."

"I bet."

"Really, they did. You want to see?" Mike jumped up from his chair and walked over to the bookcase. "Grandma keeps a photo album somewhere around here." His raised arm floated back and forth and then stopped. "Here." He pulled the book out and then, still standing, flipped through it. "Yep, this is the one."

I took the book from his outstretched arms and set it on my lap. He *was* a cute baby. His blond, shaggy hair had once been a head full of golden curls, and he had this really sweet dimple. "Oh my God, you *were* adorable," I said. Much cuter than my baby-self, though I didn't say that.

"I was fat," he said, but I could tell by his grin that he knew he was cute, then and now.

His baby photo was at the back of the album. I flipped to the front page to see an ancient black-and-white wedding photo. "Your grandparents?" I asked, turning the book so it faced away from me. When Mike confirmed my guess, I returned the album to my lap and looked again. Mrs. Bittner was much older now, of course, but you could still tell it was her. Her husband, the late Mr. Bittner, had been bulky with dark hair, like Scott.

I paged through the book, past vacation photos and miscellaneous photos of people I didn't know. They were dancing and boating, always with a drink in their hand and a smile on their faces. Mike got up and stood next to me, so we were looking together. I flipped forward in the book, losing interest in the party pictures, until I came to a studio shot of three children, two boys and a girl, all dressed in their Sunday best. Below the photo was written, "Michael age 8, Laura age 5, and Scott age 2." I looked up at Mike, questioning.

"That's my dad and his brother and sister," he said matter-of-factly.

"There's a sister? Your grandmother never mentioned it."

"She died of leukemia when she was pretty little. Five or six, I think. She was the only daughter and my grandmother's favorite. Grandma had a nervous breakdown after she died. No one ever talks about Laura because they don't want to upset her."

I ran my finger underneath the names, stopping at *Laura*. "Did you know Laura is my mother's name?"

"Yeah, I think I did know that," he said.

"Don't you think that's kind of a weird coincidence? My mother and your aunt, both with the same name?"

"It's not really an uncommon name. I'm sure a lot of girls were named Laura back then." His train of thought was clearly on a different track than mine.

I hesitated, not wanting him to think I was crazy, but needing to say what was on my mind. "Do you think the fact that my mom's name is Laura was one of the reasons Scott became obsessed with her?"

Mike saw what I was getting at now. He shook his head. "I'm not really seeing it, Angie. Look at how little Scott was in that picture, and Laura died not too long after that. Chances are he didn't even remember her. And they never talked about her, my dad said. Even as a little boy he knew not to bring up his sister's name."

"Still, it's kind of a big coincidence." My mind ran through the possibilities. Even if no one mentioned his sister, Scott must have known about her. Most of the time kids knew far more than their parents thought they did. Kids listened at doors, looked through cabinets and drawers. If nothing else, Scott would have seen photos like this one. It wasn't hidden. Mike had found it right in the bookcase. So it wasn't much of a stretch to think Scott would have come across a photo sometime in his childhood. And then there was my mother, another Laura, also with dark hair and eyes. I couldn't quite figure out what it all meant, but I had a nagging feeling it meant something.

Chapter 18

Even after Mike put the album back on the shelf, I kept thinking about how all the separate pieces fit together. One Laura died as a child, leaving her mother devastated. The other Laura disappeared as an adult, leaving her daughter, me, also devastated. And Scott Bittner had a connection to each of them. The similarities were eerie. Again I wondered if I should share what I'd overheard in the kitchen, and again my inner voice told me no. Wait.

Mike, seeing me look troubled, started telling funny stories about his friends and all the pranks they played on each other. Normally I'd have been laughing, but now I only managed a smile. He was in the middle of telling me about an incident involving a refillable popcorn bucket at the movie theater when he stopped talking and looked over at the door. "Hey," he said, waving. "We're in here."

I turned to see a tall, lanky woman walking toward us, a grim look on her face. I'd just processed that it was Mike's mom—they had the same sort of blond California look—and that she was definitely not happy, when Mrs. Bittner walked in behind her and stopped in the doorway. I felt the tension level in the room rise from zero to way off the charts.

"Mom, this is Angie," Mike said, getting up and resting a hand on my shoulder. He was either oblivious to the trouble looming or just had really good manners. "Angie, my mom."

"Hi, Angie," she said and smiled, but only a little bit, like it was an effort. "I'm really sorry to tell you kids this, but there's been a change of plans. Your grandmother," she said, and here she spoke directly to Mike, "feels very strongly about Angie and her brother staying here until she hears from their father or grandmother. I made a good case for having them go home, but I'm afraid my hands are tied."

"Really?" Mike looked at his grandmother. "You won't let us take Angie back to her apartment? Why not? She really wants to go home."

Mrs. Bittner lifted her chin and folded her arms, but she said nothing. She had a sort of smug, superior look on her face. I got the feeling that she didn't argue; things just went her way. Or else.

Mike's mother stepped closer to us and dropped her voice to a whisper. "Mike, let it go."

"You've got to be kidding," he said loudly. "Grandma, be reasonable."

"Mike," his mother hissed, "let it go. Now. I mean it." She turned to me. "I'm really sorry, Angie. I did what I could. If you give me the right contact information, I'll do everything I can to try and reach your grandmother and father for you."

"But she doesn't want to stay," Mike said to his mother. "You can understand that this is weird, with Uncle Scott being the one who did this," he said, pointing to my wrist brace. "He put her in the hospital, for God's sake."

"I understand, really I do," she said. "But I've done all I can. There is a lot at stake here financially for us, Mike." She rested a hand on my shoulder. "I'm sorry, Angie."

I knew what she meant by saying they had a lot at stake financially. Mike had told me that his dad's business had taken a downturn and his grandmother had offered to pay his college expenses. From the look on Mike's face, I could tell he was prepared to keep arguing my case, which was really sweet, but I didn't want him to lose his tuition money on my account.

"I'll be fine," I said. "Jason is going to get a hold of my dad today, and I'm sure it will all be cleared up soon. Don't sweat it."

Mike looked worried for me. "Yeah, but—"

"She said it would be fine," his mother interrupted. She reached into her purse and pulled out a small notebook and pen. "Angie, if you would just write down your father and grandmother's phone numbers, I'll make some calls when we get home."

I took the pen and paper and explained about my grandmother's cruise. Jason and I had been told we couldn't call the ship, but Grandma had said she'd check her e-mail when she could.

"If you know the name of the ship and the cruise line, I'll see if I can call and have her paged," Mike's mom said. "If it's possible to reach her, I promise you I will."

When I finished jotting down the information and handed back the notebook, she leaned over and quietly said, "I'm so sorry. Really I am." She glanced over at her mother-in-law, who was glowering at us from the other side of the room.

"I'm fine," I said. "We'll get this worked out. My brother said he'd take care of it. My dad will be calling any time now.

Mike gave me a hug good-bye and whispered in my ear, "Don't worry, I'll be back." For the brief moment his arms were around me I felt a sense of security, but it was over all too quickly.

Mrs. Bittner said good-bye to Mike and his mom as they walked past, but she made no move to see them out. A moment later, the mean look melted off her face and she smiled at me. "So, Angie, I hope you're feeling well. Would you like to take a nap before dinner? Or maybe you'd like to watch a little television?"

"No, actually," I said, "I was hoping we could talk. I have questions about Scott and my mother."

She nodded knowingly. "I had a feeling about this. Let's go up to my room and chat. I have some things to show you. I think seeing them will help you understand." I followed her to the elevator and down the hallway to her bedroom. She closed the door behind us and motioned for me to sit in a wing chair in the corner. "So, who's been telling tales about Scott and your mother?"

"I don't really want to get into that." I settled into the chair, prepared to stay as long as it took to get to the truth. "I just want to know everything. I want to know what Scott did to my mother."

"Scott didn't *do* anything to your mother," Mrs. Bittner said indignantly. "My son was mentally ill, but he wouldn't hurt a fly. He was very gentle and kind."

I didn't know what to believe. When we'd first met she'd said Scott was troubled, and I'd seen his violent side first-hand. Now she painted a completely different picture. Gentle and kind? It didn't fit. "I was told Scott was obsessed with my mother. That he spied on her through windows and called our house. It's not much of a stretch to think he had something to do with her disappearance." With her *murder* is what I was thinking, but saying that word out loud was hard for me to do.

"You make him sound so terrible, but you don't understand. Wait, I want to show you something." Mrs. Bittner opened a dresser drawer and produced a key ring, which she held up for me to see, and then she knelt on the floor and reached underneath the bed. She grunted and strained; I watched her back end shift until I thought the seams of her pants might give way. Finally I heard the scrape of something metal move slowly across the hardwood floor. Before long a metal box emerged, hingeside first. "Aha," Mrs. Bittner said, spinning the case around and wiping the edge of the dusty surface with the bottom of her shirt. "I keep everything Scott had about your mother in here," she said, inserting a key and jiggling until each latch opened. "I'm the only one who has the key," she added.

She raised the lid and I craned my neck to get a better view, but all I saw was a mass of yellowed newspaper clippings. "Why is it locked? Is there something secret in there?"

"Not secret," she said, lifting the photo album and sitting beside me. "Just personal. Scott used to get in his moods and go through all my belongings and try to take his things back. I wanted to preserve his artwork, you see. Sometimes when he wasn't in his right mind, he would rip up his sketches and photos. I wanted to save them." She shook her head. "I believe in locking up my treasures. It's important to keep what is precious close to you, Angie. Remember that." Resting a hand over the contents of the box, she said, "I call them my treasures because this was who he was." She looked past me. "And now that he's gone..." Her voice broke. "I don't have much of him left. Some pictures, my memories, and this."

"What exactly is *this*?"

Mrs. Bittner looked at me with sad, soulful eyes. "You want to know what Scott had to do with your mother. When you see what's in this box, you'll understand. Look." She stood up and carefully laid out pages on the bed one by one. I got up and watched as she covered the surface with newspaper articles, photos, and sketches of my mother. The pictures were taken from a distance: Mom getting out of the car at the Piggly Wiggly, Mom sitting on the front porch of our old duplex, Mom and me coming out of my elementary school. The sketches were close-ups—multiple charcoal drawings of her face from all different angles. She looked so much like me. So many times I'd heard that, but these sketches brought it home.

There was a lump in my throat. "Scott did these?" I pointed to the drawings.

She nodded. "Didn't he do a beautiful job? He was such a gifted artist. I think he captured her perfectly. Most people shied away from him because of his size and his awkwardness, but she was kind to him."

I felt the muscles in my neck and shoulders stiffen. The display on the bed looked like obsession, but she made it sound so sweet. "This looks like something a stalker would do."

Mrs. Bittner put a hand up to her heart and leaned forward to meet my eyes. "Some people might think that, Angie, but you have to understand that my son was an innocent at heart. He was incapable of violence," she said, sighing heavily. "I want you to know that Scott didn't hurt your mother. If anything, he was protective of her. He would have died before he let anything bad happen to her. You have my word on it."

"How do I know what you're saying is true?"

She reached over and clasped my hand. Her skin was papery and cold, but her grip was firm. "I promise you it's the truth. Believe me, Scott did not kill your mother."

I pulled my hand away. "Okay." Maybe she actually believed it, but I wasn't sure I did. Was it possible that Hank and Trudy were talking about something completely different? A crime unrelated to my mother? Anything was possible. I didn't know what to believe anymore. Mrs. Bittner and I were both still, the quiet punctuated by the chiming of a clock down the hall.

"Would you like to keep one of the sketches, or maybe one of the photographs?" she offered. "I'd gladly give them up since they are of your mother."

"No thanks," I said. "I have pictures."

What I didn't have was her.

Mrs. Bittner was totally messing with my head. She chattered on about Scott's things as if I would find it all so charming. I scanned the newspaper articles but didn't find out anything new. They all seemed to agree that my mother had disappeared without a trace. Her car was found in the back parking lot at her work, but she never went inside, and no one had seen her arrive that morning.

I found myself staring at the sketches and photos. One of them, a picture of Mom and me leaving the grocery store, really hit me hard. In the photo I was wearing my favorite pink shirt at the time, topped with a denim vest. A denim vest—what was I thinking? It had been my favorite outfit back then, believe it or not. My mother wouldn't let me wear it more than once a week. In the photo my head was tilted up like I was listening to something my mom was saying. We both looked happy. I wondered what we were talking about.

How weird that even while we were living our lives—my mom going to and from work, me and Jason going to school—all that time Scott Bittner was lurking in the shadows, following my mother, his camera lens aimed at her. Did she know he was there? Was she really friendly to him, the way Mrs. Bittner claimed? I imagined that might have been true. She was kind to everyone—the cashier who was having a bad day, the neighbor kid with the messed-up home life, the washing machine repair man—everyone who crossed her path, really. I could see her being kind to this awkward, hulking man. It was such a disturbing feeling knowing that someone had preyed on her good nature and violated her privacy.

I almost asked Mrs. Bitter if I could have the picture of me with my mom, but I didn't want her to know Scott had produced something of value to me, so I set it back on the bed and blinked back tears. I couldn't decide if I was more angry or sad. Both emotions welled up inside of me. I was also tired and couldn't make sense of any of this. All I could do was wait until we got out of there and file a police report. Maybe the authorities could get to the truth. "I think I should rest," I said, swallowing hard. "My foot is starting to hurt again."

Mrs. Bittner said brightly, "Well, of course, Angie. I'll see you at dinner then." As I walked out of the room, she lovingly gathered up all of Scott's artwork and photos.

———

By the time Jason came back later in the afternoon, I had my belongings packed and was ready to go. He let himself into my room and closed the door behind him. "Hey, Ange, how're you holding up?" Misty jumped off the bed and sidled up to his leg. Out of habit he reached down and patted her head.

"Jason, thank God you're here. Did you talk to Dad?"

He straightened up. "Yeah, about that." He had this look, the kind of look that said I wasn't going to like his news.

"What?"

"I did get hold of Dad, and he begged me not to call Uncle Bob or anyone else. He doesn't want Grandma to know he left us alone."

"You've got to be kidding."

"It gets worse," he said. "I talked to Mrs. Bittner on the way in, and she won't let you go anywhere without permission from Grandma."

"Can't Dad tell her it's okay with him?"

Jason shook his head. "She said since Grandma is our legal guardian, it would have to be her."

"How does she even know Grandma is our legal guardian?"

The expression on his face told the whole story. "Umm, I didn't mean to tell her—it just slipped out."

"Jason, what are you, completely brain-dead? This is unbelievable."

"Angie, I'm so sorry. I have no idea how it happened. Mrs. Bittner just talks in circles and goes on and on asking question after question, and before I know it she's got me saying things I don't even want to say. I already feel terrible about messing up. Getting mad at me doesn't help."

I sighed. He was right. Getting mad at him didn't help. We were in this together, after all. I told him what happened with Mike and his mom and about the conversation I overheard between Hank and Trudy. "It's so weird how Mrs. Bittner's determined to keep us here. I feel like no matter what we do we're stuck."

"Just for a little while." He sat next to me on the bed and put his arm around me for the first time in years. It was bizarrely comforting. "Dad said he'd get on the next available flight and come here from the airport. He'll be here by tomorrow morning at the latest." Another night in this house filled with dark shadows and freakish people? We'd wandered into a Tim Burton movie and couldn't find our way out.

"I'm ready to just walk out of here," I said, on the verge of crying, "even if I have to limp all the way home. It's ridiculous that we're even here. Wait until I tell you what Mrs. Bittner showed me today." I told him all about the photos and sketches and how she showed them to me as if I would find it charming, instead of disturbing. "She is really one sick lady. This whole house is crazy."

"Shh," Jason said, looking at the door.

"I don't care who hears, Jason," I said. "No one in their right mind would stay here another night. Give me your cell phone."

He reluctantly took it out of his pocket. "What are you going to do?"

I grabbed it off his outstretched palm. "I'm going to beg someone to come pick us up. I don't care if Dad gets into trouble. Grandma will be mad, and then she'll get over it. Mrs. Bittner can't keep us here against our will. If we walk out, what is she going to do?"

"You won't be able to text," he said. "It only works for calls."

"Why?"

"I don't know. It's been broken for a while. I just haven't gotten around to trading it in. It's probably because I've dropped the thing about a million times." I gave him a glare, and he said, "Angie, it's not like I did it on purpose. Things happen." Did I mention he's supposed to be this genius guy? I really think we need to change how we measure intelligence in this country.

The only friend's phone number I knew by heart was Shawnee's. When I reached her she was in Door County for the weekend with her aunt, so she couldn't help, but she gave me a few numbers of other friends. Most importantly she listened in fascination to my story. "If I were home, I'd drive right over," she said. "You know that, right?"

I did, but it didn't help. My next call was to my friend Jenna. She was willing to help but couldn't because she was grounded. Her dad had caught her with beer breath and an empty Heineken bottle in the back seat. Frankly, I was very disappointed in Jenna. So sloppy. "I'm sorry, Angie," she said, and she did sound sorry, not that it helped. After that, I got voice mail for the rest of my friends; I left messages asking them to call me back *right away*. When I finally got through to Uncle Bob's house, Aunt Carla answered. I tried explaining the situation to her, but she cut me off midsentence, saying she was on the other line and she'd have Bob call me back. By the time I'd gotten through leaving messages I was pretty discouraged, and I took it out on my brother. "This is your fault, Jason. You were all, 'Let's just go and see what she has to say about the scholarships. One dinner, how hard could it be?' Now look where we are."

"I know," he said, "coming here was a bad idea."

"A really bad idea."

Jason cleared his throat. "But just for the record, you didn't have to go on the boat ride, which is sort of what led to us having to call the doctor and then staying overnight."

"I probably shouldn't have gone on the boat ride," I agreed and sighed. I'd only done it because Mike was cute. That part of the whole thing was paying off, but I still didn't want to stay another night.

"We'll get through this," Jason said, something our grandmother always said. It made me homesick for her. Oh, how I wished she were home. I'd taken her for granted, and now everything was all screwed up.

"Just promise me if we wind up staying that you won't leave me here again," I said. "I can only handle it if you're here." I looked up at him through tear-filled eyes. I hated crying, and lately I seemed to be doing a lot of it. "Promise?"

"I'm not going anywhere, Angie, don't worry. It's just one more night, and then Dad will come, and we'll be out of here first thing in the morning. In the meantime, let's just be nice. She said the scholarships are a sure thing, and we don't want her to change her mind."

That would be my brother, always the practical one. Even in the depths of hell he was thinking about funding his education.

Chapter 19

I kept Jason's phone right next to me, waiting. When it rang a half an hour later, it wasn't one of my friends returning my call. It was Dad. "Hey, Angie, how're you feeling?" he said, skipping right past the hello.

"Fine, except for being stuck here." I got up off the bed and motioned to Jason, who'd heard the phone and come in from his room to see who it was. I mouthed the word *Dad*, and he nodded and leaned against the doorframe, waiting for his turn to talk. "When are you getting back? We're dying here."

"I'm so sorry about that, Angie. Honest to God, I had no idea." It was hard to hear him through the static and loud music in the background.

"Okay," I said grudgingly. He was always so sincere; it was hard to stay mad at him.

"Did Jason tell you my news?" Before I could answer, he said, "Just a minute." I kept the phone snug against my ear and waited. Whatever he did quieted the music, but it did nothing to improve the connection. "Is that better?"

"Yes, it's better," I said.

"I moved out into the hallway. We're listening to some other bands. Did Jason tell you my big news? I told him not to, but I bet he did anyway."

"About you coming back early?"

"What?" He was shouting now.

I repeated myself, a little louder this time.

"No, I mean about the band. Good news, baby girl—one of the network guys loved one of my songs. They're thinking of using it for the beginning of a show they're developing."

"What kind of show?" I asked.

"I'm not sure yet, but isn't that great? It could mean a lot of money, and really get us known. The network guy said it fit perfectly. I asked him who has the last word on picking the songs, and he said his vote carries a lot of weight."

His voice was muffled but exuberant. It was great to hear him so happy even if I didn't quite understand what he was talking about. I asked, "What kind of network are you talking about?"

Dad answered my question—at least I think he did—but I didn't hear his explanation because he faded out and then came back again. "I'll tell you the whole story when we get back," he said the next time his voice came through clearly. "I'm leaving from here in about an hour to go to the airport. I'll get on the next flight and come for you guys as soon as I can, I promise. I have a lot to tell you."

"I have a lot to tell you too, Dad. I think I know what happened to Mom. I think Scott Bittner—" *Crackle, crackle, crackle.*

"I'm sorry, I can't hear you at all, Angie girl. I'll see you guys soon. Love you."

"I love you too, Dad."

There was more static, and then I thought I heard him tell me to hang in there before he said good-bye.

"Good-bye," I whispered, "and hurry." I redialed the number so Jason could talk to him, but we only got his voice mail.

Chapter 20

We ate dinner in the formal dining room and used the good china and crystal that had been in Mrs. Bittner's family for generations. The salad included some greens I didn't recognize, topped by pine nuts and chunks of avocado. I almost turned down the main entrée, which was veal, because all I could think of was a wide-eye, adorable calf, but I ate it anyway. It was delicious. In all fairness, I was really hungry.

"This is nice, having company for dinner," Mrs. Bittner said, smiling, and I had the sickening feeling she'd keep us with her forever if she could. She asked so many questions, it was like being interrogated. She wanted to know who our friends were and what we did for fun. Later the talk turned to nosy questions about Dad and my mother. How did they meet? Where did they get married? Did we ever see their wedding photos? So weird. Jason and I exchanged glances, and it was understood between us that we weren't giving away much on that subject. "I don't know too much about that," I said. "It all happened before I was born." Jason claimed not to know anything either, which seemed to disappoint her.

Mrs. Bittner served champagne, which Jason drank and I didn't. She made a big deal out of it, and when I politely refused, her eyebrows raised. "Not even a sip, Angie?" she said. "Oh, I wish you would. I think you'd really enjoy it. It's very refreshing and not strong at all. My boys often drank this with dinner when they were about your age." She held the bottle above my empty glass and let it hover there, waiting for me to give in and say okay, but I was too smart for that. She reminded me of the witch offering an apple to Snow White, and I knew how that story ended.

"Actually," I said, "I signed a no-drinking pledge at school, and I'm determined to see it through." Jason smirked at my lie, and I thought he might say something, but he held back, thankfully.

"All right then," she said, in a way that let me know I'd let her down. During dinner, she compensated for my lack of champagne by adding to Jason's glass whenever it got even a little bit low. He didn't seem to mind.

After dinner we made excruciating small talk until Jason saved the day. "I'm really tired from working all day, and I think my sister needs her rest too," he said. "Thanks for the nice meal. I think we'll be heading upstairs." I breathed in relief. All we had to do was lock ourselves in our rooms, and Dad would be coming to get us in the morning. Just one more night, and if we were together, nothing bad could happen. Soon this would all be over.

"But it's so early," Mrs. Bittner said. "I was hoping you kids would want to play Monopoly or watch a little television with me." She exhaled in a huff, the way little kids do when they don't get their way.

"Thanks," Jason said firmly, "but I promised my dad I'd look after Angie, and she looks really tired. I think we both need to get our sleep."

"I am really tired," I said, managing an awesome fake yawn so good it triggered an actual real yawn. "Thank you for dinner.

It was delicious." She looked so pitiful I almost felt sorry for her. But it only lasted a minute, and then the feeling was gone. Sorry, Mrs. B.—you can keep us here, but you can't make us play board games.

———————

Back in our rooms, I checked the phone and found nothing. "I can't believe no one called back," I said to Jason.

He shrugged. "It's Saturday night. People are busy."

"Yeah, it's Saturday night, but come on; I said it was a matter life and death." I'd begged even. Wait until one of them needed a favor. I'd probably still do it, but I'd make them feel bad by reminding them of the time they let me down. I shook the phone. "Are you sure this thing is getting incoming calls?" If the texting function was broken, it wasn't too much of a stretch to think the whole thing was shot.

"It worked when Dad called just a little while ago," he said. "You should know—you were the one who talked to him."

Finally Jason and I gave up and went to bed. Knowing Dad was coming in the morning helped. I was just sinking into the realm of almost-sleep when the puzzle pieces of my phone conversation with Dad came together. *A network show.* That's what he'd said and I hadn't understood, but now my brain was clicking and a realization startled me to wakefulness. A television network, a television show! Now it made sense. Of course that's what he meant. I'd been thinking in terms of record companies and band shows, but of course it was possible that other media big shots were checking out the bands as well. I wondered if it was a cable network. And were they considering Dad's song as part of one episode or as the theme song for a series? I tried to remember past theme songs and could only come up with a few. I couldn't name any of the musical groups behind the songs, but that didn't mean someone hadn't made big bucks doing it. I wished I'd gotten more details. Now I'd have to wait until he got back.

Now that I was awake, I said my usual nightly prayer for my mother, trying to send vibes out to wherever she was in the world, but tonight I couldn't feel her. My connection had been broken. I blamed Mrs. Bittner and the negative energy of the house. Every room was beautiful, filled with dark wood and marble floors and crystal chandeliers, but instead of being lovely, it was oppressive. The longer we stayed, the more I felt like the walls were draining me of energy and hope. I prayed again, and this time I wished for an answer. *Please God, help me find out what happened to my mom.*

I stared wide-eyed at the ceiling for what seemed like hours. Despite the fact that I thought it was a good idea to lock the doors leading to the hallway, I suddenly felt trapped. My foot throbbed and my heart started racing, but I practiced my breathing techniques and talked myself through it. Maybe I should have had some of that champagne after all.

I finally fell asleep, only to be awakened abruptly at two in the morning. A wailing sound roused me, a noise like a baby crying or maybe—here I sat up and really listened—a cat mewing in distress. Misty? But she was right in the room with me, and this sounded far off. I turned on the nightstand lamp. "Misty?" No answer, and I couldn't see her. "Here kitty, kitty, kitty." I listened but didn't hear the noise that had awakened me. Had I dreamt it?

When I got out of bed, I winced from the pain of my once again tender ankle, proving that the doctor was right—I should have rested it. Walking on it all day had aggravated the sprain. Grabbing one of the crutches, I walked through the bathroom into Jason's room. "Jason," I said, pushing on his shoulder. "Where's Misty?"

"Don't know," he said, without opening his eyes or moving a muscle.

"When did you last see her?" I didn't remember spotting her when we got back from dinner, but she loved hiding under beds and behind furniture. I'd figured she'd come out when she felt like it.

"Don't know." He rolled over to face the wall and pulled the covers up to his chin. My brother was clearly not going to be any help.

I heard the yowling again, this time coming from outside our rooms. "Do you hear that?" I hissed at Jason. "Misty got out, and something's wrong."

He flapped a hand. "So tired, Angie. Can't this wait?"

It could not wait. I opened the hall door and stuck my head out, listening. I heard Misty crying again, this time farther away. What was going on?

I saw a movie once where a killer lured a woman out of hiding by playing a tape recording of her child calling for his mother. I sat in the theater watching the screen and willed her not to follow the sound. Every fiber of my being begged her not to go, but in true movie fashion, not only did she come out of hiding, but she did it calling, "Hang on, baby, Mommy's coming!" as she moved through the house. Talk about making yourself an easy mark. This was what was on my mind as I left Jason's room, but still I went. Misty was my cat, the baby I'd had since third grade. I had to go.

I grabbed my house key, which had a mini-LED flashlight attached, and left my room as noiselessly as possible, using just the one crutch. I stood in the hallway for a moment, letting my eyes adjust to the darkness. I could have flipped on some lights, but I hesitated, not wanting to alert Mrs. Bittner. All I wanted was to find Misty and bring her back to my room. My guess was that she'd slipped out when we came in and was now lost.

Out in the hall I still heard Misty's wailing, but it wasn't as continuous. Still, when she did cry it was frantic, making me think of the word "caterwauling" and how some words just sound like what they mean.

Slowly I eased toward the noise. When I reached the end of the corridor by the staircase, it was clear Misty was somewhere above me. I stood on the landing beneath a patch of moonlight coming from the octagonal window. Her crying was heartbreaking.

"Misty?" I whispered, trying to project my voice without getting any louder. I hoped she would come to me. "Misty!" I know it sounds silly, but the next mew I heard sounded like an answer.

"That's it, come on down," I coaxed and then switched on the flashlight. I heard the scampering of her little cat feet and then meowing from the top of the steps. By my estimate, we were only a flight of stairs apart. I could tell she was close, but the curve of the staircase kept her out of view. "Come on girl."

I heard her there, and then she was gone. Instead of coming down to me, she receded further, and now she was yowling and carrying on like her tail had gotten caught in a door.

I said her name again, a little louder this time, but it didn't seem to make a difference. She didn't return.

I didn't see or hear anything that made me think someone was with her. It seemed like she'd climbed the stairs and was freaked out about coming back down. She could be weird like that.

With the flashlight still aimed in front of me, I backtracked down the hallway and took the elevator to the third floor. It would be a miracle if Mrs. Bittner didn't wake up. Thankfully, she'd consumed a lot of champagne. That would help.

Up on the third floor, I kept the flashlight on as I crept down the hallway in the direction of the meowing. Misty was close by, but still not responding. I followed the sound to the end of the corridor.

All the doors I passed along the way were closed. I swung my flashlight back and forth in front of me like metal-detecting at the beach, but Misty wasn't in sight. It wasn't until I reached the very end that I realized she'd gone higher yet. There was a half staircase that let up to the fourth level, the towers. I'd admired the huge towers with their stained glass windows from outside, but I never actually thought I'd be going up there.

And I really didn't *want* to go up there. I had no desire to drag my body up the steps. I leaned against the wall to rest. "Misty, Misty, come on girl." I said it several times, changing the intonation each time, but the cat wasn't budging. As much as I wanted to retreat to my room and go back to bed, I'd come too close to leave now. Where the hell was Jason when I needed him?

I didn't realize I was holding my breath until I exhaled. The cat wasn't the only one who was freaked out. "Misty?" I whispered. She mewed again. Now I was certain she'd climbed the stairs to the tower level. Damn. I made a clicking noise with my tongue that she'd never responded to before, but for some reason I thought it might work in this case. It didn't. "Misty, come on now. Let's go get a treat." I really should have brought her treats with me. It was always so easy to think of these things after the fact.

She poked her head out at the top of the stairs, her eyes glowing in the flashlight's beam. But it was only for a second, and then she was out of sight and crying again.

I grabbed onto the railing and hoisted myself onto the first step. I rested and then maneuvered myself up to the next one. I wished I'd had the presence of mind to look for a light switch— my flashlight and the moonlight through the windows helped, but I was still working under pretty dark conditions. When I got about halfway up, Misty started screaming like a cornered baby bunny. Her crying gave me a boost of adrenaline. I took a deep breath and worked a little harder. It was stuffy up here and warm, and I perspired from my efforts, but I kept going.

I got to the top of the stairs and shone the light on the floor, where Misty sat looking up at me. "Why did you make me come up after you, you bad girl?" I looked around to get my bearings, while she paced a figure eight pattern around my legs. I was standing at the end of a long hall, with a single door in front of me. I assumed the door led into one of the two towers. I turned the knob, but it didn't budge. I swung my light onto the wall to the left of the door and gasped when I saw what looked like a person. A second later I was relieved to realize it was just a painting of a woman in old-fashioned clothing. A Bittner ancestor, no doubt. Similar portraits hung all down the hallway. On the opposite wall stood a floor-to-ceiling glass-front curio cabinet, which held the visor from a set of armor and various old-timey swords and battleaxes. The whole setup reminded me of the haunted houses my friends and I went through at Halloween. Too creepy.

While I was peering through the glass at the swords and axes, Misty disappeared again, this time farther down the hall-way. Oh man, I felt like I had run a marathon. Still, I crutched in her direction. Maybe she'd killed a mouse and I could admire her prey and we could be done with this nighttime expedition.

At the end of the hallway was another door and, thankfully, a window that let in some moonlight. In front of the door, Misty sat grooming herself in the fastidious way cats do, her determined pink tongue flicking at her paws. You'd never have guessed that she'd just made such an enormous fuss.

"Let's go, Misty," I hissed to the cat. My head throbbed at the temples, and my good leg was unsteady. A feeling of dread came over me suddenly, and I just wanted to get back to Jason. I leaned over as far as I could and tried to pick up the cat, but she jumped away from me and started screaming again. Really screaming—it was bloodcurdling, actually. I rested my hand on the doorknob and leaned against the door. Too bad the elevator didn't come up to this level. I didn't look forward to the walk down. "Be quiet!" She was trying my patience.

I was tired and hot and sick of my cat. I loved her with all my heart, but even so I considered leaving her on the fourth floor until tomorrow. Even better—I should go and wake up Jason, who had two good legs and could easily scoop her up and carry her down.

After deciding that, yes, waking my brother *was* the best plan, I turned back the way I came. But I stopped when I heard something above the noise of Misty's yowling—a clicking sound and then a voice. Misty stopped too and cocked her head as if listening. There it was again—the sound of a doorknob rattling and someone speaking. A woman's voice, from behind the door. "Is someone there?" she called out. I froze and then heard her again. "Please, who's there?"

I turned back and called out, "Hello?"

"Yes, who is it?"

It wasn't Mrs. Bittner's voice, I knew that much. Then I heard the sound of a lamp being switched on and saw a sliver of light underneath the door. Oh my God, this was freaking me out. I got closer and spoke to the door. "I'm just a guest staying for the night. I'm sorry my cat woke you up. I've been trying to get her to come back with me."

"No, no, please don't leave." I could tell by the way the door shifted that she was leaning against it. "I'm locked in. Will you help get me out?"

"You're stuck inside?" I shone my light and saw an old-fashioned keyhole underneath the knob. "I can go and ask Mrs. Bittner for the key."

"No, don't do that!" The knob shook from the other side. "They've locked me in here. I've tried and tried to get out, but nothing works. Please help me."

It was those last words that went through me like an electrical charge to my heart; the familiarity of the voice clicked in my brain. I put my hand on the knob, knowing that her hand was on the other side, the metal connecting us. My breath was caught motionless in my chest. I exhaled and wondered and hoped and prayed all at the same time. I gulped. "Who are you?" I asked, silently praying as I said the words.

"Laura Favorite," she said hurriedly, not knowing that I'd been begging God to let me hear that exact name. "Oh please, please help me before one of them comes."

Chapter 21

"I'm Angie." I was so overcome with emotion that it was hard to get the words out. "Your daughter. Angie." I swallowed hard. "Angel Marie."

There was a long pause. "Is this some kind of trick?"

"No, no, it's really me." I wiped tears from my eyes. And then a rush of words came to mind, everything I'd wanted to say to her for the last five years. "All of us—Dad and me and Grandma and Jason—we looked for you. We didn't know what happened to you, but we never stopped looking. I used to—"

"Can you just open the door, please? Hurry." The sound of her voice fell lower with each word like she was sliding down to the floor, and then she started to cry—loud, heart-wrenching sobs.

"I'll get you out, Mom. Even if I can't, Jason has a cell phone and we can call 911." She didn't answer, just kept crying, but I didn't pause for a response. I stuck my apartment key into the keyhole, but not surprisingly it didn't work. Damn. If only I carried a Swiss Army knife like Dad. Certainly that would do the trick. I pushed against the door and wondered if Jason could kick it in. It was so massive, I sort of doubted anyone could force it open, but maybe he'd have another idea. "I'm going to get Jason. I'll be right back, okay?"

"Don't leave me, please don't leave me," she said frantically. "Don't go. You have to help me." She banged on the door with what sounded like her fist. "Please."

"Don't worry, I'll be right back. I promise I'm not leaving you." I tried to sound confident even as I wondered exactly how I was going to pull this off. The door seemed impenetrable. The how and why of her imprisonment was only a fleeting thought at that point. I was running on pure adrenaline. After five years apart, all I could think of was how to get to her.

I needed to find something big and heavy. Something big and heavy and forceful enough to get through a locked door. I was almost to the other end of the hall, Misty at my heels, when I had a brilliant thought. Everything I needed was in the large, medieval curio cabinet I'd just passed. I backtracked and shone my light into the case, illuminating enough weaponry to penetrate any door. The cabinet was locked though, which was only a problem for a second. "Get away," I warned Misty, and she did. I took one step back, raised the crutch, and shattered the glass.

The sound of it breaking was loud enough to raise the dead.

I reached in and pulled out a battleaxe. It was heavier than it looked, and I had to drag it down the hall. At that point I didn't care how much noise I made. Hopefully Jason would wake up before Mrs. Bittner, but even if she confronted me, I was pretty sure I could stand my ground. Having a battleaxe in hand gave a person confidence. "Mom," I said once I reached the door, "I'm back."

"Good. Oh good." Her voice came through the keyhole.

"I have an axe," I said. "I'm going to try to break the door down, but you have to move back. I don't want you to get hurt, okay?"

"Okay." I heard some shuffling from behind the door, and then she said, "Go ahead."

I leaned on the crutch and swung the axe as high as I could until it made contact with the door. It sort of bounced off, barely making a dent, so I swung again, this time changing the angle and raising it higher. The stupid thing got stuck in the door. "Damn," I said under my breath. I pulled on the handle, but the blade was wedged tight.

"What is it?"

"It's caught in the door," I said. "Stuck."

"You should try hitting at the doorknob," she said. "The wood is solid; I don't think you'll be able to get through it."

I wished I'd thought of that. "I'm going back to get another axe or something," I said. "I'll be back." This time I got a shorter, lighter, bladed thing—a hatchet. My arm was tired, but my determination was strong. I called out another warning before I started hitting at the doorknob. The first few blows only made noise, but on the fourth try something inside the lock mechanism rattled and the knob loosened. I paused to wipe my forehead, and then I started whaling away at it, using every ounce of my strength. When the knob on my side finally came loose, it flew off with a startling force and the door shook in its frame. At the same time, the battleaxe came loose and thundered to the floor, narrowly missing my feet.

I stood still for a moment and watched as the door slowly swung open.

Chapter 22

She looked tiny compared to how I remembered her. I almost thought it was someone else. Her floor-length nightgown was unlike anything she'd ever worn at home, and her hair was longer. When my eyes adjusted to the light, I recognized the way she reached up to brush her hair away from her face, and we made eye contact. At that moment I knew.

It was my mother. Yes, it was.

"Mom, it's Angie." I said. "I'm Angie."

"Angie? It's really you?" she said. I stepped over the axe and closer to the light so my face was visible. She smiled in recognition, and her expression was sheer amazement, as if I'd materialized from nowhere. I went to give her a hug. We were the same height now, and she was so thin I was afraid I might hurt her if I squeezed too hard. When she stroked my hair the way she always did when I was upset or sick, I knew it was real.

"Oh, Angie." Her sigh was a wisp of air next to my ear. "I've dreamed of seeing you so many times. All this time, I've been praying. Months and months and months. I don't even know how long it's been."

I pulled away and looked into her eyes. "You've been gone five years, Mom."

"Oh God." She put her hand up to her mouth. "That's why you're so tall. How old are you now?"

"Sixteen."

"Sixteen," she repeated slowly. "And Jason and your father—what about them?"

"Except for missing you, yes, we're all okay," I assured her. "We didn't know what happened to you. How did you get here?"

"Your father and Jason—they're okay?" she asked softly.

"Yes, yes, they're fine."

"And my mother? Grandma?"

"Grandma's fine too. She's on a cruise right now."

Mom let out relieved sigh. "Oh thank God, it was a lie, just like I thought. She told me you were dead. All dead, she said, and she was the only family I had left. There was a car accident. You all died. She showed me a newspaper article and waved it in front of my face. I could read the headline, but she didn't let me read what it said." She wiped her eyes with the back of her hand. "I didn't really believe you were all dead, but there were some days...well, let's just say I prayed a lot."

"Who said we were dead? Mrs. Bittner?"

Mom looked nervously down the hall. "I'll explain later. We have to get out of here right now, Angie." She was beginning to sound frantic. "I got out one time, but then they stopped me. We have to go, *now*. We don't have time to waste."

"Okay," I said, "but we have to go down and get Jason. He's still sleeping."

"They have Jason too?" Her voice broke, and she clutched at my arm. "Oh God, oh no."

"No, it's not like that," I said. "He's not locked in. We're staying here as guests." Seeing her confusion, I added, "I'll explain later. It's complicated." We made our way down the hallway, me limping and Mom trailing hesitantly behind. When we got to the weapons case, my crutch was against the wall right where

I'd left it. I handed Mom the flashlight and retrieved it, sticking it under my arm.

"You're injured?" Mom asked, worry in her voice.

"Just a sprained ankle," I said. "I'll be fine."

When we reached the stairs, she led the way while I followed, leaning on the railing. We were on the third floor now. I took comfort in the fact that Jason was sleeping just one level below. "We can take the elevator," I said, pointing. I crutched slowly in that direction, Mom's hand on my shoulder, like she was afraid of losing me again.

We were within arm's reach of the elevator, so close I could taste safety, when the ceiling light in the hallway flicked on, making me blink at the sudden brightness. Mom's hand on my shoulder tightened, and I felt my throat knot up.

Mrs. Bittner stood at the other end of the hall, her hand on the light switch. She strode toward us with a large ring of keys in one hand. "And what do you think you're doing?" The shrillness of her voice put a shiver up my back.

"We're going home," I said and turned to push the elevator button. I waited for Mom to say something, but she just looked down at the floor.

"You're not going anywhere," she said. "This is my house. I say who stays and who goes."

"It's not up to you," I said. "We're leaving." I was ready to hit Mrs. Bittner with my crutch if she tried to stop us. It wasn't a battleaxe, but I thought it would do the trick.

"Laura," she said harshly, "you know you're not well. Go back to your room right now. I don't want to have to tell you twice. I mean it. I know what's best."

I felt Mom's hand quiver on my shoulder, but she didn't say anything. Mrs. Bittner changed to a nicer tone of voice. "Laura, you know I love you and that you've always been my favorite. You don't know this girl. She makes all kinds of claims, but I wouldn't trust her if I were you. You've seen the documents. We have the photos. This is your family. You are a Bittner, and you belong here. We take care of you. Don't listen to a word this girl says. She's a liar, and she's trying to confuse you."

The elevator creaked up to our floor, and the doors slid open. I said, "Get in, Mom." My mother backed into the elevator, her eyes on Mrs. Bittner the whole time. I'd thought Mrs. Bittner would try to follow us or keep us from getting in, but she just stood there twirling her keys, a satisfied look on her face. Right before the elevator doors slid closed, Misty appeared out of nowhere and, like Indiana Jones, slipped inside at the last second. We'd made it.

Chapter 23

My heart was pounding. What a close call. "It's okay, Mom," I said as the elevator slowly descended. "I'm getting you out of here. We're going home."

"I want to believe it," Mom said, "I really do, but I've just got such a bad feeling." She shook all over, like it was bitter cold in the elevator instead of stiflingly warm.

I wanted to give her a reassuring hug, but I had to stay vigilant in case Mrs. Bittner was waiting for us when we arrived on the second floor. "It's okay. It's going to be all right." The elevator rumbled as it slowly descended.

"I just have such a bad feeling," she repeated. In the light of the elevator, I could finally get a good look at her. She was gaunt. Her eyes had dark circles beneath them, her hair was disheveled, and her skin was pale, like she was the ghost of my mother.

"I'll get you home. I promise." What could Mrs. Bittner do against the two of us? Three of us if you counted Jason, and I did since he would soon be awake. The odds were in our favor.

I gripped the crutch, ready to use it as a weapon when the door opened, but I never got the chance because we arrived with a thud and the doors stayed firmly shut. "What's going on?" I waited and exchanged a glance with my mother, who looked terrified. There wasn't a button for opening the door, so I pressed the number two button again. Nothing happened. "Why isn't this working?"

I was really just thinking aloud. I knew why it wasn't working even before my mother said these chilling words: "She controls everything."

"Let us out," I yelled, slamming a fist against the door. As if in response, we started moving, this time going up and then stopping. As far as I could tell, we were now halfway between the second and third floor.

Mrs. Bittner's voice echoed from above. "I say who stays and who goes."

She sounded so vicious a chill went down my back. In fear I hit at the door with the side of my fist, making as much racket as a jackhammer. "Jason," I screamed. "Jason, wake up! Jason, we need help."

"He's not going to hear you, so there's no point in yelling," Mrs. Bittner called down. "No one will hear you." I heard the jangle of keys. "I'll come back in one hour to check on you, and there'd better be an improvement in your disposition, or else."

Or else what? I looked to my mother for advice, but she wasn't offering any. "That's it then, I guess," Mom said, wrapping her arms around me. "It was a good try, honey."

"We're not done here," I said, stepping out of her embrace. "There has to be a way out." I slammed the crutch against the door, and when that didn't work, I pushed all the buttons on the control panel. "Help," I screamed. "Someone help us!"

"Shhhh, you're just going to get her mad." Mom stroked the back of my hair. "Save your strength. There's no point in getting all worked up."

No point in getting all worked up? How could she want to give up when we'd come so close? "It's okay, Mom. Jason is going to hear us." Why he hadn't already was a mystery, but he had to eventually. "Even if he sleeps through this, he has to come looking for me when he gets up in the morning. And Dad is going to be here to take us home. It's not like they'll leave without me."

"You don't understand how she is, Angie. She's probably done something to Jason already—locked him up or knocked him out or something. Then when your dad comes they'll say you two aren't here, that you left on your own or something."

I thought back to the dinnertime conversation and how Mrs. Bittner kept asking us questions. I'm sure she'd heard enough to put together a pretty convincing lie. She could say that Shawnee came to pick us up in her Mustang, or that Jason's boss, Roger, had come by in his truck. Would Dad suspect Mrs. Bittner of lying? Probably not—he was pretty trusting. "But maybe when Trudy comes in the morning to make breakfast she'll hear us and—"

Mom shook her head. "She's part of this too." She leaned back against the railing. "They're all in it together. No, we're trapped."

"Why is this happening?" Nothing made sense. This was insane. A horrible nightmare come to life.

"Let's sit down. I'm kind of tired," Mom said. "We might be here until morning, and then they might separate us. I want to look at your beautiful face while I still can." She reached up and patted my cheek.

"Don't you think we should be making noise so Jason can hear us?"

"He would have woken up already if he was going to. We can try again in a few minutes if you want." She slid down to the floor and sat with her legs extended. "Come sit with me."

Mom patted the floor next to her, and I obediently joined her. Misty, sensing some female bonding, jumped into Mom's lap and rubbed her head against Mom's hand. "Good old Misty," Mom said. "At least she's the same."

"Tell me what happened," I said.

She put her arm around my shoulder, and I nestled my head against her like I used to when I was little. This moment was the good dream inside of the nightmare. "The last thing I remember from home was that it was your birthday, remember?" I nodded. It wasn't a day I'd ever forget. I recalled everything about my eleventh birthday perfectly, including the taste of the chocolate cupcakes my mother had made. In my head I had replayed every detail a million times. Every birthday afterward felt like a funeral.

Mom told the whole story simply and quickly, summing up the last five years in just a few minutes. She'd arrived late to her job at the dentist's office that morning because of the cupcake stop at school. When she got out of the car, she'd felt light-headed and dizzy. Scott Bittner drove into the parking lot just then and called out of his car window to ask if she was okay. That was the last thing she remembered before she passed out. When she woke up, she was on the couch in the Bittner living room.

"He knocked you out," I said, putting together the pieces, "and then kidnapped you."

"Oh no," she said. "It wasn't his fault. I really did faint and hit my head on the pavement. The car had an exhaust leak. We kept meaning to get it repaired." She shook her head. "I usually drove with the windows open, but that day I was in a hurry to get to work and I don't think I was as careful. I must have inhaled some fumes."

No one had ever mentioned a problem with the exhaust. You'd think the police would have found that to be an important detail. Come to think of it, I don't think anyone ever used my mother's car after she disappeared. I didn't know what had happened to it, but I knew it was gone. I needed to hear the rest. "But he *did* take you—and keep you."

"No, that would be the mother," Mom said softly. She explained that Scott lifted her up and put her in the back of his car and took her home because he wasn't sure what else to do with her.

"It didn't occur to him to call for help or go to a hospital?"

"No, he wouldn't have thought of that. He's a very simple person."

None of this was making sense. Mom was portraying Scott as simple, but well intentioned. He brought Mom to his house, the castle, but that wasn't the problem. "The problem," my mother said, "was his mother. Lillian was overjoyed to see me. She was convinced that I was her daughter, brought back to her. Scott kept telling her I was Laura Favorite, and his mother kept saying Laura *was* her favorite. I didn't understand what was going on at the time. I sat on her couch with blood dripping off my forehead and said I had to go, that they were expecting me at work. I wanted to use the phone, but she insisted on cleaning up my gash herself and giving me a cup of tea. She said I should drink the tea before I even thought of doing anything else. There was something in the cup—I know that now. When I woke up, I was in one of the bedrooms and the door was locked from the outside."

"And then she kept you here *for five years?*"

She nodded. "I didn't know it had been five years. It seemed like forever, but I never really knew how long it had been." She was quiet for a minute and then continued. At first, she said, she thought they'd certainly let her go. They had to let her go. Keeping a grown woman against her will was ludicrous. She begged and pleaded, told them she had children and a husband at home who would miss her.

They drugged her food to keep her sleepy, something she figured out after a few days. She overheard Scott pleading with his mother to let her go, crying about it, in fact. And she heard Mrs. Bittner telling him, "Laura belongs here now, with us." My mom shuddered at the memory. "She told Scott that he'd done the right thing, bringing me home. That it was meant to be." Mom said Scott tried calling his brother Michael to tell him his mother had me here, but Hank grabbed the phone and told them Scott was off his meds and delusional. After that they kept tabs on Scott and disconnected the house phones except for the one in Mrs. Bittner's room.

Mom continued, "At some point after that, Scott disappeared and no one would say where he went."

I thought about Mike telling me that Scott went off to a residential treatment center. Even if they shipped him away, why hadn't he told anyone his mother was holding a woman prisoner in the family home? Or maybe he'd tried but they hadn't believed him. How did Lillian Bittner get away with this?

"She controls people by lies and threats and promises," Mom said, as if answering the question I'd been thinking. "After a while you don't know what to believe. And day after day she wears you down until you lose all hope."

"But why would Hank and Trudy go along with it?"

Mom shook her head. "I don't know."

I thought about what I'd overhead Trudy say to Hank in the kitchen that morning about keeping a secret and waiting for a payoff. *She promised the big payout at the end of the year. We get the money then and we're gone. Hang in there for just a little while longer.* My mother was the secret, the blackmail that would allow them to walk away rich.

I remembered something else Trudy had said. "Mom, Trudy said Mrs. Bittner has a gun. Did you ever see it?"

She nodded.

"Did she ever shoot anyone?" I asked.

"I never saw her shoot a person," my mother said softly, "but she once killed the neighbor's dog out in the yard. She told me to watch from the window. I didn't know she was going to do it. It was horrible." Mom looked really shaken.

"Why would she do that?" I asked, incredulous.

"The dog kept coming over onto her property. And she wanted to show me the gun worked." She turned her head, but I still saw her blink back the tears. "She had some meat, which she threw on the ground as a lure. She called the dog, and it came running up—" She paused to wipe at her eyes with her fingertips. "And then she shot it right in the head and smiled this hideous smile." My poor mother. I stroked her hair like she did when I was upset as a little girl. Mom shuddered at the memory, but once she regained her composure she continued, telling me she never saw anyone besides Mrs. Bittner, Hank, and Trudy. Hank never spoke directly to her. She only knew his name because Trudy had a tendency to talk. "They put something in my food that makes me tired," she said. "I tried not eating, but I couldn't keep it up for long."

Sometimes they let her go downstairs and eat meals with the rest of them. Often she'd watch TV or play Scrabble with Mrs. Bittner. Once in a while Mom played the piano and sang for her. Mom said it made life easier to just go along with whatever

Mrs. Bittner wanted. "She said I should call her Mother. I wouldn't at first, but eventually I just got so tired I gave in. I thought she might let me go if I went along with whatever she said, but she never did. In the beginning, I tried to get away every chance I could," she said. "But this place is a fortress. And every time I tried, it got worse for me afterwards. Eventually, I stopped trying. But I never stopped hoping."

"I was praying for you," I said. "Every night. I prayed to God you would come back to us."

"I know." She wrapped her arms around me. "It gave me hope." We sat quietly for a moment, and then she continued. "When Scott returned not too long ago, I knew he would help me. They didn't tell him I was still up here, but he figured it out. We spoke through the door, and he was on my side. We had to do it all very hush-hush. The only time they let him go anywhere alone was for walks around the lake, so he had to be very sneaky when he went into town. Sometimes one of the neighbors gave him a ride. He wouldn't go to the police because his mother had put the fear of God into him when it came to that, so I told him to go look for my family. He came back and said your father had moved and my mother didn't live at the old house anymore..." She stopped and cleared her throat. "He didn't know where you kids were or what happened." She sighed. "I almost gave up hope, but then one day Scott came to the door and told me he'd seen you walking on the sidewalk one day when Hank was driving him to the dentist. He was pretty certain it was you, said you looked like me. I wrote a note for him to give to you, and off he went. He said he'd keep looking if it took him the rest of his life. And then he found you and told you where I was," she said, smiling. "And you came for me."

Chapter 24

I had a sick feeling in my stomach. Scott wasn't trying to attack me after all. In his own misguided way, he'd been trying to help. *Come with me*, he'd said. *You need to see something.* I could have cried thinking of how he came after me and how I struggled to get away. What happened to the note she gave him, and why didn't he just hand it to me? He'd been my mother's one hope, and I'd run from him, sure he was trying to attack me, when really he'd been desperate to get me to go with him. And because of me, he went to jail. And now he was gone, the one person who had tried to help my mother. I felt awful.

I wasn't sure how I would tell my mother, who clearly didn't know that Scott was dead. I was still thinking this over when the light in the elevator went off. My mother shivered in the darkness and said, "Oh no, she came back."

We waited. "I don't think so," I said. "It hasn't been an hour yet. The light must go off automatically after a certain period of time." We both listened to the silence. "No, she's not back yet." The dark closed in around us, and even with my mother right at my side, I felt the familiar dizziness and quick heartbeat that preceded the panic attacks I'd had before. We were trapped in a small, stuffy, enclosed space. I hated that feeling. What had the nurse said? Breathe in, breathe out, slowly, slowly. And Michael at the restaurant had talked me through it, using pretty much the same advice. I inhaled slowly and carefully and willed my heart to slow down. *Air in, air out, just relax*, I told myself. Easier said than done, but it seemed to be working. Yes, it *was* working. I was actually heading off a panic attack. Yay me.

In the dark my mother cupped my chin with her warm fingers. "Now I can't see your beautiful face."

"I'm really not beautiful."

"You are to me."

I continued with my measured breathing until my heart rate slowed down to business as usual. I felt in control, or at least in control of myself, if not the situation. Being stuck here reminded me of my dad's story of getting trapped in the service elevator with his band. He'd had a similar panic attack, but hadn't handled it as well. Of course, he didn't have the benefit of instruction from a nurse, like I did. How did Dad's story end? Oh yeah, he said the elevator didn't even have an escape hatch, so they had to pry the doors open with a crowbar. Wait. An escape hatch? Was he talking about one of those trapdoors in the ceiling of an elevator? "Mom," I said, sitting up, "is there some kind of exit panel in the ceiling of this thing?"

"There was, but someone painted it shut," she said. "I don't think it works anymore."

"Do you still have the flashlight?"

"Right here," she said, fumbling in the dark. When our hands connected, I felt the familiar shape of my key ring pressed into my palm. Thank God for my smart grandmother, who'd insisted I have a flashlight attached to my keys. "You never know when it will come in handy," she'd said. Amen to that, Grandma. I clicked the light on and aimed it at the ceiling. Sure enough, there was a square the size of a doormat in the center of the ceiling. The outline was faint, as if someone had caulked around the perimeter, but it was definitely there.

I stood up. "I'm going to try something."

"Oh Angie, do be careful."

I raised the crutch over my head and pushed against the trapdoor. It wiggled a little, but didn't move. I looked down at Mom. "I think to get it loose I'm going to have to hit it pretty hard. Can you hold the flashlight for me?"

She grabbed the railing and pulled herself up. "I'm not so sure this is a good idea, Angie. If you ruin the elevator, she'll be very angry. I've seen her when she gets mad, and it's not good. Usually I just try to play along—"

"Mom." I put a hand on her shoulder. "We're going to get out of here. She can get as mad as she wants in jail." I sounded more confident than I felt, but one of us had to be strong, and I could tell Mom didn't have it in her. I handed her the flashlight. "Stand back and aim the light right on it." Now that I had two hands free, I could really get some leverage with the crutch. I raised it above my head and repeatedly pushed against the door as hard as I could. *Bam, bam, bam.* With every hit I made headway, and the square got looser.

Next to me my mother was saying, "Oh, I don't know about this, Angie. I have a bad feeling." The light shook a little, but she kept it aimed right at the spot.

"It'll be okay," I said. "Really, we'll be fine." I gave one final shove, and the panel burst free and clattered somewhere above us. Bits of dust and plaster rained down on us. Blech. I could taste the dust. As the air settled, Mom shone the light directly into the opening. We could see nothing. It looked like the black hole of death in one of Jason's games, something smart people avoided. "I'm going up," I said.

"Oh Angie." I couldn't see the expression on Mom's face, but her tone was worried.

"Can you give me a boost?"

"Are you sure you want to do this? What if the elevator starts up again?"

"Then I'll just jump down," I said. "Don't worry, Mom. I'll be fine."

Mom reluctantly linked her hands into a stirrup, and I stepped in using my good foot. My other ankle still throbbed, but that was the least of my worries right now. Using her help and pushing off the crutch, I was able to get up to the opening and stick my head and shoulders through. Talk about dark and musty and spooky. This was a real-life black hole of death. Mom gave me an added push, and I pulled myself up and through, releasing the crutch, which clattered to the floor. The only light came from the flashlight below, which Mom handed up to me. "Be careful up there, honey."

I knelt down and took the flashlight from her hands. Once I could stand, I used the light to get my bearings. The shaft was quite a bit wider than the actual elevator. One wrong step to the side and I could have dropped straight down to the first floor. I didn't mention this fact to Mom, who was still calling out for me to be careful. Ahead of me, at waist height, was the door to the third floor, complete with lever. Standing on tiptoe, I was able to push the lever. The door didn't open, but it clicked like I'd released something, and I manually pulled the two doors apart. "I've got it," I called out. "I've got the door open to the hallway."

"Oh honey, be safe." Mom's voice from below was hushed. "She's going to be back any minute." Misty mewed what sounded like a little cat warning.

I knelt down and stuck my face in the opening. "I've got the door open, and I think I can boost myself up. I'll go for help and come back for you." I lowered the flashlight to her, but she didn't take it.

"Oh don't leave me here," she said. "She's going to come back soon, and if you're gone..."

"Mom, take the flashlight." I waved the beam of light at the floor, and she took it reluctantly. "And if she comes back, hit her with the crutch. I promise you I'll be back. I promise." I would have pulled my mother out and taken her with me that minute if I had the strength, but I didn't. The best I could offer was my word.

I got up and leaned through the open doors, and then I pushed off and crawled out into the hallway of the third floor. "I'll call for help," I whispered down into the hole. "And then I'll be right back."

Chapter 25

Now what? I wondered if finding Jason was my best bet, or if I should just leave the house, hobble down the road to a neighbor's house, and ask to use their phone. Under normal circumstances, I'd have picked my brother, but it was odd that he hadn't heard us yelling for help. What if he was drugged or locked up somewhere and I got trapped along with him? What good was I to Mom then?

But if I left the house, I'd have to get past the gate or go around a fence that seemed to go on forever. And what if Hank or Trudy saw me outside and tried to stop me? My ankle was starting to really hurt again, and I was barefoot. I didn't have a weapon and couldn't outrun anyone. There was no good answer.

Afraid to switch on the light, I started slowly down the hall, making my way by the moonlight that came through the small window at the opposite end. When I got to the stairway, I went down one step at a time, leaning heavily on the railing. At the second floor, I hesitated only a moment and kept on. I decided not to look for Jason. In horror movies that was a fool's game. *Get out now*—that was the right strategy. Better to go for help.

When I reached the first floor, I heard voices coming from the parlor where we'd first met Mrs. Bittner. It was a man and a woman. I stopped to listen. Nope, not a man—my brother Jason. I exhaled in relief. He was fine, or at least fine enough to be out of bed and talking. I listened some more until I identified the other voice as Mrs. Bittner. I almost called out to my brother, but something made me wait. I moved as silently as I could and got closer to the doorway.

"You're all worked up," Mrs. Bittner was saying. "You need to calm down. Just finish drinking your tea, and then I'll get Hank and we'll do a thorough search of the house. It's a big house, Jason. I'm sure Angie just couldn't sleep and is off reading somewhere."

"But it so weird that the cat is gone too." Jason's speech was slurred. My guess? There was something in the tea. "Maybe we should call the police. Angie really wanted to go home..."

"Angie wouldn't have left in the middle of the night with a bad ankle," Mrs. Bittner said soothingly. "We'll find her. Don't you worry about that."

"I'm so tired. I just..." Then I heard the sound of a cup and saucer crashing to the floor. "Sorry," my brother murmured.

"Don't you worry about that," she said. "You're tired, I can see that. Why don't you just lie down right there. That's a good boy. Just sleep. I'll take care of everything."

I backed away and crossed the hall into the knitting alcove, hoping she wouldn't see me. I knew I could take her. She wasn't very big and I had the element of surprise on my side, but I still didn't want a confrontation. For all I knew, Hank was somewhere in the house and would rush to her aid. When she finally came out of the parlor and walked by, I held my breath. If she had turned her head one fraction of an inch she might have spotted me, but lucky for me, she didn't.

Once she was safely past, I left my hiding spot and went to my brother, who was curled up on the sofa. "Jason," I hissed. "Wake up."

He opened one eye. "Angie. Oh. Good. You're. Okay." His eye closed, and he settled back in to sleep.

I got right down next to his ear. "Jason, listen carefully, this is *very* important. Mom is here. Mrs. Bittner has been keeping her prisoner. We need to go for help. Get up. Get up now."

"Mom?" he muttered.

"Yes, Mom is here. You need to get up." I poked him hard, I mean really hard, and he grunted, but that was his only reaction. Oh man, he wasn't going to be any help. Whatever she gave him was fast acting. I looked back at the doorway, afraid Mrs. Bittner or one of her minions would find me. If she'd gone from here to the elevator, she might have already figured out I'd escaped. I poked my brother one more time, and reflexively he pushed me away with his closed fist. As he did, I saw a glint of metal and realized his fingers were wrapped around something. His cell phone. "Oh Jason, I love you so much. Give me your phone." He groaned, but let me loosen his fingers, one by one. Thank you God, and also thank you whoever invented cell phones.

I flipped it open and was ready to call 911, but then it rang. Jason's ring tone was the music from his game. I answered it quickly and quietly. "Hello?"

"Angie, what are you doing up at five in the morning?" It was my dad. My eyes welled with tears of relief. He said, "I was just going to leave a message for Jason."

"Dad, you won't believe this. I found Mom. She's here at Mrs. Bittner's. They've been keeping her prisoner and—"

"Hold on, Angie, you're talking so fast I can barely keep up. What about Mom and Mrs. Bittner?"

"Mom's here, Dad, but she's trapped in the elevator and I can't get her out. I'm going to hang up and dial 911, and you need to drive straight here as soon as your flight gets in. If you get here and Mrs. Bittner or Hank or Trudy says we're not here, they're lying. Don't trust any of them."

"Angie, is this real?" I heard his voice catch in a funny way.

"Mom is really here, Dad. I've seen her. I've talked to her. I've hugged her. Mrs. Bittner told her we were dead and—"

"I'm at the apartment. I'll be right there, Angie."

I said, "Hurry, Dad, I love you," but he'd already hung up.

I punched in 911 with shaking hands. The dispatcher seemed a little unsure of what crime I was reporting. In our small town they were used to break-ins and theft and domestic abuse. I was pretty sure that a woman held against her will for five years was a new one. Still, the dispatcher sounded like she believed me. She took all my information and said, "I'm sending officers to the scene, Angie. Stay on the line with me until they arrive. We're going to get you through this. Just be calm; someone will be there soon."

Having her voice in my ear was reassuring. She instructed me to unlock the front door and open the gate, but I couldn't do either. These doors weren't like the ones at home. There was a deadbolt that required a key. Besides that, some kind of security system was in place. How it all worked was beyond me. "I don't know what to do," I said and started crying.

"You don't need to do anything. Officers are on their way," the dispatcher said. She sounded nice, like she was someone's mom. "Don't worry, help will be there soon. You're going to be fine."

"Okay," I said, wiping my eyes.

"Now, you said your mother is trapped in an elevator?"

"Yes." I gulped air and sniffed. Poor Mom, I hoped and prayed she was okay. "Should I go and tell her the police are on their way?"

"No, stay right where you are. The squad cars will be there soon. When the officers arrive, they'll know how to proceed."

Squad cars, officers—both plural. That sounded reassuring. The dispatcher asked me more questions, and I wound up spilling out the whole story, including the part about my eleventh birthday. It sounded incredible even to me.

"You're a really brave girl," the dispatcher said. "You've been through a lot. Just hang in there. Just a little while longer."

"Thank you so much." I was sitting at the bottom of the stairs now, phone pressed to my ear, waiting. I wanted it to be over. "But how will they get in if I can't get the door unlocked?"

"Let them worry about that," she said. "They're trained to handle all situations."

Upstairs I heard a noise, like a crash. I looked up and heard a woman yelling angrily. Then I heard someone else crying out. It sounded like my mother. "Oh no," I said and stood up.

"What is it?" the woman on the phone asked.

"I don't know," I said. I heard some screaming now, but I couldn't make out who it was. "I'm hearing shouting and noises like someone's getting hurt. Oh God. I'm afraid she's killing my mother." I started up the stairs. "I have to go help her."

"Angie," the dispatcher said sternly. "Stop, right this minute. You need to stay put. The officers are almost at the scene. They'll be in the house in a minute. Let them handle this."

"I have to go. I'm sorry." I dropped the phone and went in the direction of the noise. When I got to the top of the second floor, I flipped on the light switch. At the end of the hall Mrs. Bittner stood just outside of the elevator, which was now level with the floor. When I got closer, she swung her outstretched arm and aimed a gun right at me. I halted, uncertain. Behind Mrs. Bittner I saw Mom cowering in the back of the elevator.

"You. Angie." Mrs. Bittner had a crazed look in her eyes. "Get down here. Now." She motioned with the gun for me to come.

My heart hammered in my chest, but I didn't move. "Let her go," I said. "The police are on their way. I called 911 and told them everything. It's over."

"You have no idea who you're fooling with, little girl," she said, her face turning red. "You come down here right now. You will do what I say."

"Please put down the gun before someone gets hurt," I said. "It's not too late to solve this peacefully." These lines worked in movies, but it didn't look like they were doing much here.

"I will shoot you on the count of three if you don't get down here now," she said. "I will shoot you, and I will kill you. Don't think I won't do it, because I will. I'll tell the police you were an intruder and I was defending myself."

"Let her go," I said. "Please."

Mrs. Bittner's hand shook, but the gun was still pointed at me. "One."

I took a step forward. Where were the cops when you needed them?

"Two," she yelled.

"Okay, okay, I'm coming." Please, I prayed, let someone get here in time to help. My heart pounded and I tasted bile, but I moved slowly toward her, keeping my eyes on the gun the whole time. I stopped an arm's length away from the weapon and held my hands up in the air. "I'm here. I came."

She smiled coldly. "Sorry. Not fast enough." She raised the gun and aimed it right at my forehead, giving me a view of the end of the barrel. "Three." As I heard the gun click, I saw my mother come out of the elevator. Mrs. Bittner squeezed the trigger, and reflexively I ducked. At the same moment, Mom slammed Mrs. Bittner in the back of the head with the crutch. The gun went off as she crashed to the floor. The shot was deafening, and I was jarred by the noise, but to my shock, it was just noise. I wasn't hit.

Mom looked at Mrs. Bittner sprawled face down on the floor and then stared at the crutch with wide eyes.

"Mom?" I said. "Are you okay?"

"I didn't mean to do it." She gulped and gestured at the blood on the side of the crutch. "She was going to kill you." Mom covered her mouth with her hand. "I didn't mean to hit her so hard; I just wanted to stop her."

I leaned over to get a closer look and carefully pried the gun out of Mrs. Bittner's curled fingers. "It's okay, Mom. She's still breathing." Her legs twitched, and she let out a groan. Mom had hit her hard enough to knock her out, but it hadn't killed her. I hoped she would recover enough to stand trial.

Downstairs we heard the crash of the front door being forced open, accompanied by men's voices. Even from up here I heard the crackle of their communication devices. One guy shouted, "Clear." So they actually did that in real life.

"Oh no, someone's here." Mom grabbed my arm and squeezed it hard.

"It's the police, Mom. I called them. Dad's coming too."

"Your father?" Her tone was so sweet, so hopeful. I think she still had trouble believing her long ordeal was finally over.

"Yes, he's on his way. We need to go downstairs now." I pulled her gently toward the landing, and the two of us made our way down the stairs to meet the police officers who were trained for every conceivable situation. Except no one had ever conceived of a situation like ours. I started off explaining what had happened, and Mom filled in her part. All of the police officers remembered the disappearance of my mother five years before, and here she was, a gaunt version of her former self, hair matted and voice quaking, telling an almost unbelievable story. They asked question after question and exchanged astonished glances.

At some point they let Dad in. When he walked in and saw my mother, the look on his face went from disbelief to joy. He gave her a hug and then pulled back to take a long look at her face. "Oh, Laura," he said, kissing her tenderly on the forehead. Tears flowed down his cheeks. "My Laura. What happened to you? You're all skin and bones."

She smoothed her hair self-consciously. "I know I must look terrible."

"No, no," Dad said, "you look beautiful." He held onto her like he was never going to let go.

Another detective arrived, an older gentleman with a thick middle and a gruff way of speaking. I recognized him as the one who'd questioned me at Trinity Hospital.

"Angie Favorite," he said, shaking my hand. "We meet again."

"You were at the hospital."

"Yep." He used his teeth to pull the cap off his pen then asked me some questions, pretty much the same ones the other officers had asked. "This is one for the books," he said, whatever that meant.

An ambulance came, and the EMTs took both Mrs. Bittner and Jason away. I told the paramedics about the drugged tea, and the police officers found the cup and saucer and bagged it up for evidence. When they brought Jason out on the gurney, Mom went over and traced his face with her fingertips. He didn't stir at all. "He's all grown up," she said incredulously. "My baby boy is old enough to shave." She clutched my father's arm as they wheeled my brother out the door, and I could tell it killed her to stay behind. You could see it on her face—now that she was free, she didn't want any one of us to leave her side.

My mom didn't think she needed medical attention at the hospital, but the police told her it was standard procedure. When she looked at my dad, he nodded and said he'd go with her if one of the officers would bring me and his car there when they were done questioning me. I think it was at that point that it finally sunk in for her she was really leaving the Bittner castle, her prison of five years. She started sobbing and shaking. Dad wrapped his arms around her and stroked her back. "You're going to be fine, Laura. Everything's going to be okay."

And for the first time, it seemed like everything would be fine after all.

Chapter 26

On cop shows, this sort of investigation would have been wrapped up by the third commercial break, but in real life it seemed to take forever. The entryway teemed with people— EMTs, police officers who came and went up the stairs, and at one point I saw a camera, but I never did see what they were taking pictures of. Hank and Trudy were summoned from the guest cottage, but they both claimed not to know that the lady of the house had kept a prisoner in the tower room for five years. Of course, Mom and I had already filled the authorities in on the real story.

Mike arrived at sunrise. He'd seen the police cars during his morning bike ride around the lake and came right over, he said. He looked stunned as he talked to the police. A few minutes later I heard him ask one of the officers, "Can I talk to Angie privately?"

The detective looked at me, and I nodded my okay. Once we were alone in the parlor, Mike motioned for me to take a seat. Outside the room I heard the voices of the police officers and the squawk of their radios, but neither of us spoke for a moment. I cleared my throat. "So, you wanted to talk to me?"

He knelt down next to my chair and placed his hands on the armrest. "I just wanted to tell you that I had absolutely no idea that any of this was going on. None whatsoever. If I had known your mother was in this house, I would have called the police myself."

"Okay," I said.

"And I tried calling here last night. I asked for you, but my grandmother said you were sleeping. I didn't believe her, and I even came over, but no one answered the intercom. I know I promised I'd be back later. I want you to know I tried, I really did." His big blue eyes widened in a show of sincerity.

He was waiting for a response, so I said, "Okay."

"Do you believe me?"

I thought for a minute. "Yes, I believe you, Mike." I thought I was a pretty good judge of character, and both Mike and his mom, from what little I saw of her, seemed like good, decent people.

"I was hoping," he said, maintaining eye contact, "that maybe we could stay in touch? You know that show at The Rave is still coming up, or we could get together sometime just to talk, if you want."

I looked at his kind face and remembered how he'd talked me through my anxiety attack and how much fun we'd had talking in the library. He was caring and funny and smart and good-looking. But he was also a Bittner. And I couldn't imagine ever getting past that. "I don't think," I said, finding my voice, "that's going to happen. I'm sorry." And I really was sorry. I liked him so much. If we had met at school or at a concert, we might have become a couple. I had envisioned it even, had imagined what it would be like to have him as a boyfriend, but now the association with his grandmother was too painful.

He sighed. "Okay, I respect that," he said, rising to his feet, his voice disappointed. "I guess I don't blame you. I'd probably feel the same way under the circumstances."

The fact that he was so nice about it made it even worse.

Chapter 27

I've found out that a happy ending doesn't come just like a snap of the fingers. It sometimes comes with tears and transitions and emotional meltdowns, and my family experienced all those things over the next month or so. Mrs. Bittner and Trudy and Hank were arrested and sent to jail. The prosecuting attorney interviewed my mother and Jason and me, and the trial was scheduled to come up in a few weeks. We were told that an insanity defense was a reasonable assumption. Hank cracked like an egg when questioned and admitted to everything, which was a huge help to our side. My mom is not looking forward to testifying, but the mental health professionals all say it brings closure. I think we'll all be happier when the trial is over. If I had my way, all three of them would be in prison for life, but sadly, it's not up to me.

My grandmother and Arthur flew home early from their cruise after Mike's mother called the ship and told them what was going on. After Grandma arrived home, she cried on and off for a day and a half. She wanted to hug my mom all the time, just to prove she was real. Mom came to live in the apartment with us, and the plan was that Dad would move in after Grandma got married and moved out. Frankly, I thought Grandma should move in with Arthur even before the wedding. They went on a cruise together—they must have shared a room. What was the difference, really? But no one asked me, and I didn't suggest it.

I officially declared Misty the best cat in the universe. She gets extra treats now, whenever she wants, which is all the time. She's getting pretty fat.

My mother has gained some weight too, which gives her a healthier look. She doesn't like to talk about her time away from us. Don't push her, the psychiatrist said. She needs time and love and acceptance. We'd get her back, he said, eventually. She just wasn't the same as I remembered. I missed her easy laughter and carefree ways. Now she was nervous and afraid, compulsively locking doors and checking windows. She thought her captors might come back after her, even though everyone assured her she was safe.

I went for counseling myself, and it was more helpful than I would have thought. From the outside I looked completely healed, but I was still sorting through some emotional issues. Free-floating anxieties is what Jason calls them. I had to quit my cleaning jobs because I hated working alone. Going in elevators became impossible. I was haunted by disturbing dreams. Life has changed, but it turns out that talking to some guy about my problems was helpful after all. He prescribed pills in case I got another panic attack. Just having them makes me feel better.

My dad's song sold to the television show for an unbeliev-able amount of money, making the Bittner Foundation scholar-ships completely unnecessary. My grandmother grumbled that if you spread Dad's money out over the twenty-some years he'd been a musician it still wasn't much more than minimum wage, but I think she was secretly pleased for the rest of us. Dad's music was suddenly in demand for other types of things too.

One of his songs was going to be used for a soup commercial, and another was being considered for a horror movie. Not quite the career he envisioned, but as he said, life takes funny turns. You just have to go with the flow.

I've been out to visit Scott Bittner's grave twice now. There's no headstone yet, so I had to stop at the cemetery office to find out where he was buried. When I found the spot, I stood next to the grave and said aloud that I was sorry. I thanked him for helping my mother and for doing the right thing. The first time I went I didn't experience any closure. I just felt awful—guilty and sad for how his life turned out. But the second time the sun came out from behind a cloud as I went to put the bouquet of flowers down, and I know this sounds cheesy, but I took it as a sign. I like to think that Scott forgave me for not understanding what he was trying to tell me. I just didn't know.

The morning of my grandmother's wedding, I helped my mother get ready in the changing room at the church while Grandma fussed with her makeup in the adjoining bathroom. Mom lifted her hair while I zipped up the back of the rose-colored bridesmaid gown, the dress I was supposed to have worn, back when I'd been Grandma's first choice as maid of honor. Jason said I'd been fired from the wedding party, which was fine with me. If having my mom back meant getting fired, then bring it on.

The dress was kind of pretty, though the color wasn't something I would have picked. It looked good on Mom though. "There," I said, stepping aside to look at her reflection in the mirror, "now you look beautiful."

"Do you think so?" she asked, smoothing her hair.

"Yes, I do."

I put my face next to hers, and she patted my cheek. "There's the beauty," she said, meaning me, but I took it to mean the two of us finally together. I smiled at our images in the mirror. Everyone had been right—we did look alike. "Your dad asked me if I wanted to renew our vows today, after the ceremony," she said and looked to me for a reaction. "Grandma and Arthur said they wouldn't mind."

"So you're going to do it?"

"Yes, I think we should."

So that's how I saw my parents get married all over again. I was a maid of honor that day after all, and my brother Jason got to be the best man. The sun shone through the church's stained glass windows and cast a multihued glow over my parents as they exchanged vows. Mom beamed when Dad slipped the new ring on her finger, and after the minister announced they were man and wife *again*, the congregation burst into applause. For the first time in a long time I wasn't dwelling on the past; I was enjoying the present, where all of the people I loved were reunited at last.

My dad may have been the one with psychic hunches, but at that moment I had my own vision of my family's future. And it was all good.

About the Author

Karen McQuestion has had literary aspirations since the third grade, when her teacher read her short story out loud to the rest of the class as an example of a job well done. She has been writing ever since. *Favorite* is her second novel. She lives in Hartland, Wisconsin, with her husband and their three children.